BOOKS BY

JOHN SWARTZWELDER

THE TIME MACHINE DID IT

JOHN SWARTZWELDER

Kennydale Books
Chatsworth, California

Published by:
Kennydale Books
P.O. Box 3925
Chatsworth, California 91313-3925

First Printing June, 2004
Second Printing September, 2006
Third Printing January, 2008
Fourth Printing January, 2010
Fifth Printing, May 2014

ISBN 13 (paperback edition) 978-0-9755799-0-9
ISBN 13 (hardback edition) 978-0-9755799-1-6
ISBN 10 (paperback edition) 0-9755799-0-8
ISBN 10 (hardback edition) 0-9755799-1-6

Library of Congress Control Number: 2004093998

Printed in the United States of America

CHAPTER ONE

Frank Burly is my name. Okay, it's not my name. I lied about that. My name is Edward R. Torgeson Jr. I changed it for the business. You've got to have a tough sounding name if you want people to hire you as a private detective out of a phone book. I chose one that would give prospective clients the idea that I was a burly kind of man, the kind of man who would have the strength and endurance to solve their cases for them, and who would be frank with them at all times. Hence the name.

As my exciting story opens, I am being punched in the stomach. But I guess a lot of stories start that way. Most of mine do anyway. The guy who was punching me was a lot burlier than I was, so it hurt plenty. But I tried to pretend it didn't bother me at all, that I actually liked it. It was hard to do this convincingly, because he had kind of knocked the wind out of me there, so all I could do was smile and wink and give him the thumbs up while I waited to be able to breath again. He thought I was making fun of him and

1

started punching me in the stomach harder. Meanwhile, I'm not any closer to getting my breath back. Some days are like that.

This case I was working on wasn't a criminal case or anything glamorous like that. It was just a bodyguard job. I don't like doing that kind of work. We private eyes are a proud race. But you've got to keep the old money coming in if you want to eat regularly. Which I do.

The body I was guarding belonged to an 18 year old punk named Eddie. He was afraid that some other punk was going to cause him some trouble that night, so he hired me. Kids have too much money these days, if you ask me. Anyway, he was right about the trouble. It started in a vacant lot with the usual name calling and shoving; the same kind of thing that I heard started World War I. Before things could get that bad, I stepped in front of my client to guard him from harm, as per our agreement. This is when I got my big surprise. The other punk whistled and some big guy stepped in to protect him. He had a bodyguard too. So that's how this fight got started; the one involving my stomach.

I've got to admit that my stomach is an enticing target. Not that I'm out of shape, you understand. I'm 190 pounds of rock hard muscle, underneath 40 pounds of sturdy protective fat. It's important to have that layer of fat. You can't have guys hitting you in your muscles all the time. But that extra padding also cushions the blow for your opponent's fists, which allows him to slug you longer and with more abandon. So that layer of fat is both a good and a bad thing, I guess. It works both ways is what I'm saying.

While we were beating the tar out of each other, I noticed that Eddie and the other punk were sitting off to one side watching us fight and smoking a joint. I found out later that they were friends. They had decided to hire bodyguards and watch them fight because there was nothing good playing at the theater. That kind of stuff makes me mad.

The fight was fairly even for awhile, but then the other guy got in a lucky roundhouse punch to my jaw, followed by three lucky kicks to my ribs, then he had the good fortune to step on my face. That pretty much ended the fight right about there, with the victory going to my opponent. But that's okay. You can't win them all, is a saying of mine. I'll win the next fight. Or one of the ones next month. While I was unconscious, Eddie stuffed some money in my pocket and he and his pal wandered off. Probably to see if they could start a war or a famine or something and watch that. I don't know about kids today. Television's to blame, I guess. Or radio. Some kind of broadcasting.

It was pretty late when I woke up. I felt the money in my pocket, pulled it out, counted it, and grunted with satisfaction. I had taken bigger beatings for less money, so I didn't really feel like I could complain. Besides, there wasn't anybody around to complain to. I had been out for quite awhile apparently. There were some soft drink containers on me that had been tossed there by passing motorists. I've been told by people that I'm shaped kind of like a garbage can, but I don't know if that's the truth, or just some kind of an insult. Anyway, it would explain all the soft drink containers. Also I noticed there was a rabbit hiding under me. So I must have been laying there quite awhile. I decided to get out of there, maybe get something to eat.

I know people reading stories like these want to know all the little intimate details about guys like me. What we like to eat and where we like to take a crap and so on. So, for the record, when I sat down at a nearby diner, I ordered a ham sandwich with all the trimmings. And since it was payday for me, I also ordered the fries-of-the-day. In fact, I announced, fries for everybody. There were only a couple other people in the place, so the gesture didn't cost me much.

While I was eating, I thought I saw something strange out of the corner of my eye. It looked like one of the patrons sitting in the back booth kind of shimmered and went out of focus a little. In fact, the whole booth shimmered. When things had stopped shimmering he had a stack of hundred dollar bills in front of him and a 3 day growth of beard.

Now, I'm not the most observant of men, which is unfortunate, because I'm a private eye. I'm supposed to notice things. It's my job. People pay me large sums of money to notice things on their behalf. When I don't notice enough things, these same people yell at me that they're going to give me X amount of more chances to notice things or

I'm going to be replaced by Y or Z, whatever comes into their minds to replace me with. But sometimes I get lucky and actually see something that's going on. This was one of those times.

The guy who had been doing all the shimmering and beard growing saw me looking at him, felt his chin, then put on a pair of sunglasses.

Something weird is going on, I thought to myself. Right here in the diner. I decided to investigate.

I walked over to where the guy was sitting. He quickly closed a briefcase he had open in front of him, which made me kind of wonder what was in it.

He looked up at me. "Yeah?"

"Could you do that again?" I asked. "That suspicious movement you made there a minute ago? I missed most of it. All that shimmering and going out of focus, I mean. Let me see that one again."

"You a cop?"

I handed him a card. I had cards printed up saying I'm a private eye, so I guess until someone prints up some cards saying I'm not, I am.

He looked it over with contempt. "Snooper, eh? Get lost."

He tore up the card and threw it on the floor. I winced. If he knew how much those cards cost he wouldn't tear them up like that. He wouldn't frame them or anything. They're not that valuable. But he wouldn't tear them up. But it was my fault for giving it to him, I guess. We live and learn, I've noticed.

6

I got lost as requested and sat back down at the counter. I asked the guy behind the counter if he had seen anything weird.

"Every day, pal," he said. "You want to see life in all its permutations? Work behind a lunch counter."

He started recounting all the weird things he'd seen, starting from about 1973. I tried to get him to fast forward a little to more modern times so we could get to the thing I was asking about, but you know lunch counter guys. One story reminded him of another—mostly because they were all exactly the same—and pretty soon we were back to 1973 again. My head was still hurting from my recent beating and I'd heard the lunch counter guy's stories before, so I finished my coffee and left.

I wasn't interested in looking into it any further anyway. Call me disinquisitive, if you like, if there is such a word, but if what I had seen in the diner was part of some fascinating seemingly insolvable crime, I didn't want any part of it. The thing about fascinating seemingly insolvable crimes is that they don't pay any better than crimes you can understand. You've got to pick and choose in this business is all I'm saying.

The kind of case I like is where I've just deposited my retainer in the bank and I turn around and there's the missing person I've been hired to find and I say something like 'hey your horseshit wife is looking for you' and he says something like 'No kidding! Thanks for the tip.

I'll call her up right now'. And the case is solved. That's the kind of case I like.

The next morning I parked my car in the garage and took the elevator up to my office to start what I hoped would be a good day. I try to maintain a positive attitude at all times, because clients notice little things like that, and if you're frowning and crying all the time and saying "why? why?", they get worried. So I try to stay upbeat.

The words on the door to my office said "Frank Burly Private Investigations." I looked at it with pride. Not everybody has a door with his name on it. Though I suppose everybody could. Paint's pretty cheap. But I was proud anyway.

I entered the office and paused in my reception area (not everyone has a reception area) to talk to my secretary, Elizabeth Squirrel. She was reading one of those love magazines that tell you what love is like.

"Any calls?" I asked.

She didn't look up from her magazine. "What am I, your secretary?"

"Yes."

"Look, just leave me alone."

I went into my inner office and sat down at my desk. I wondered if I'd had any calls.

When I started my business I tried getting one of those wisecracking secretaries who is everybody's pal and a good egg and practically solves all the crimes by herself, like those secretaries they have in the movies, but I couldn't find any secretaries like that around here. They're probably all in Hollywood, making movies and important wisecracks. The one I have is worse at cracking wise than I am. But I figure when you hire the cheapest secretary you can find—when you base your hiring choice on price alone—this is what happens.

I looked around my office with quiet satisfaction. The place looked pretty nice. I had pictures on the walls of me posing with clues, getting yelled at by the mayor, and so on. There was a calendar on one wall that was running a couple of years slow, but it looked okay and had the months right, so I left it up. On another wall was a sign that said "DO IT TOMORROW". I got it cheap because it's bad advice.

I had been a detective for about four years at this point. Before that I had just had regular jobs. Those jobs that burly men get; lifting things, carrying things, keeping things from rolling any farther, jobs like that. Then one day I had seen an ad in a magazine that hinted that I might just be the guy the exciting field of crime detection was looking for. You could have knocked me over with a feather. I got out a pencil and took their simple and fun detective test and it determined that I had the interest to become a serious student at their school. So I quit my job, rented an office, and sent away for their mail order detective course.

This will probably surprise you as much as it did me, but the whole thing turned out to be a scam. Yes it did. The first couple of lessons taught me how to dress like a detective and spell "detective", but the last 38 lessons were just torn up newspapers. I could have gotten those anyplace. I didn't need to wait for them to show up in the mail.

This experience would probably have turned some people off from the detective business just when they were getting started, but after I had spent two months tracking down the guy who ran the school and then forced him to give me my 3 dollars back, I started thinking maybe I did have what it took. Solving crimes is hard tedious work. It's not for everybody. But I am a hard tedious guy. Once I get started doing something, I can't think of anything else to do. So I keep at it. This made me think I should give the detecting game a try. And here I was four years later, still giving it a try.

It's tough to make a living in my racket. Most people who need detecting done just go to the cops. They're free. I have to charge money for essentially the same service. Another thing that makes it tough is that I'm not the best detective in town. In fact in this building you have to pass the offices of three detectives who are better than me to get to my place. So I guess I lose some business that way.

But I don't blame people for going with the more qualified detectives. Let's face facts here. If you're in a hurry to have some crime solved you shouldn't come to me. I mean, if that's all you want out of a detective is a quick solution to your problem, maybe you'd be better off hiring someone else, because solving crimes is hard for me. That doesn't mean I'm stupid. Not at all. Of course, it doesn't mean I'm a genius either. It could go either way. We need more information.

When I first opened my office, I tried to increase my business by putting an ad in the phone book that had a snappy slogan underneath my burly looking picture. Something like "Eye See That Thing You're Looking For" or "Eye M A Detective" or something like that. Maybe with a picture of an eye on there. Or an animal. But it never sounded right and I didn't want to promise too much. I didn't know how much people could hold you to legally about promises made in phone books but I didn't want to chance it. And I can't draw an eye anyway.

On this particular morning, I didn't need any crazy publicity stunts like advertisements to increase my business. Two prospective clients walked in the door within the first 45 minutes. The first one came in hesitantly, as if hiring a detective was not an everyday experience for him, like he was afraid he might get hurt somehow. I was anxious to make him feel comfortable. I slicked back my hair and invited him to sit. Sit, by all means. Sit all he wants.

"Your name Burly?" he asked.

"Sort of."

He sat down and told me his story. There had been a burglary at his home two nights before. All that was stolen was a new mailbox he had recently purchased and lovingly pounded into his yard. He wanted me to investigate and, hopefully, get the mailbox returned to him unharmed. He said the police weren't interested because it was "only a mailbox". His voice was shaking a little when he told me that.

I indicated that I had some free time at the moment and was willing to investigate what sounded like a most important case.

"How much do you charge?" he asked.

"$500 a day, plus expenses."

"Will the expenses make it less?"

"Possibly, but in my experience expenses usually add to the total."

He thought about this for a moment, then frowned. "Well, I suppose I should just forget about it then. Spending $500 a day to find something worth $20 wouldn't make economic sense."

"That's true, if it's just the money you're concerned with here and not the justice angle."

"No, it was the money more than anything else. I guess it would be cheaper to just buy another one."

I agreed that this was probably so. He got up and left, and aside from the occasional Christmas card, I never heard from him again.

I was about to write off the morning as a total loss and take an early lunch, maybe go to that new all-you-can-eat spaghetti place downtown. I usually come out ahead in all-you-can-eat places. They underestimate how much I can eat. But just when I was starting to wonder just how much spaghetti I could eat, another prospective client came in.

Looking back on it, the mailbox case would have been easier.

CHAPTER TWO

He was a scraggly smelly specimen, looking even less promising than most of my clients, but he breezed in like the Secretary Of The Treasury.

"I am Thomas Dewey Mandible The Third," he announced.

He seemed to think that was a name that should create a sensation in my office. That I should faint dead away upon hearing it, or call the newspapers and tell them to hold the front page because guess who was in my office. But it didn't create much of a sensation. In fact, I was a little disappointed he'd come in right at that moment. I asked him if he wanted to go get some spaghetti with me, we could talk over his problem there, while we were seeing how much we could eat, but he wasn't hungry.

I sighed and motioned for him to sit down in my client chair. Since he seemed so aristocratic I was glad I'd decided to designate the best chair I had—the one that didn't violently fall over periodically—as my client chair.

"What can I do for you, Mr. Mandible?"

He informed me that he was a multimillionaire, the wealthiest man in the city. I looked him over with a skeptical eye and made a discrete snorting sound. He bristled.

"What is the meaning of that snort, young man? Don't I look like a wealthy man to you?"

"Yeah, I guess so. Kind of. But you look more like a tramp. Or maybe a maniac."

For a moment it looked like he was going to sock me. But that would have been inadvisable. He might have had the style, but he didn't have the weight. I guess he realized that because he quickly calmed down and told me what had brought him here.

He said he had been a multi-millionaire when he had gone to bed the night before in stately Mandible Manor, but somehow during the night he was robbed of everything he owned: his money, his clothes, his house, bank accounts, stocks, everything he had in the world was gone.

"I woke up this morning in a cardboard box, which I was told to get out of because it wasn't mine."

"Sounds like a very serious robbery you had there." I said.

"Yes." He brooded for a moment, then continued: "But none of that is important."

"No. Of course not. I can see that." I made a circular motion with my finger around my temple to indicate I thought this guy was crazy, forgetting that there was no one in the room to see this circular motion except him. He saw it and frowned.

"That is to say, it's important, but it need not concern you. I will handle the recovering of my fortune. But during the robbery I also lost an item of enormous sentimental value to me. That is what I want you to find."

He handed me a picture of a figurine about twelve inches high of Justice Holding The Scales: that statuey-looking thing you see when you're watching one of those courtroom dramas on TV. The figurine didn't look very valuable to me. I guess he could see that in my face, and hear it in the raspberry I blew.

"It has no monetary value, as you have guessed," he said "but it was my family's most prized possession. It belonged to my grandfather. Get it back for me and you can name your own price."

I thought about his story, and consulted my notes. I realized I couldn't read my notes, and had forgotten most of his story.

Sometimes my clients have to explain their problems to me more than once. I don't charge them for that. It's part of the service, I figure. If the case is really complicated, I might ask a smarter detective, or the guy who runs the elevator, to sit in and simplify the whole thing for me. You can't be vain about these things. You can only bluff your client for so long, then you have to admit you didn't understand what he was talking about and you've forgotten his name, and to please start again. And the longer you put off admitting it, the madder he's going to be. I made Mandible run through his story again. He was mad, but like I said not as mad as he would have been later.

I studied the picture of the figurine he'd given me. "I could probably find your house easier."

"Just the figurine, Mr. Burly. Find that and you'll have earned your fee."

"Who do you suspect? Who steals from you normally?"

He said his family had always had trouble with a group of idle low-lives called "poor people". Ever since Mandible Manor was built poor people had been plaguing it; squatting on the extensive grounds, stealing fruit from the trees, and so on. Some of them even lived in the walls of the manor itself. You could hear them at night, sometimes, when they scuttled out to play the piano.

"It might have been one of them. Or it could have been one of those pest control people I bring in periodically to spray for poor people. Or it could have been just a common burglar. But that's what I'm paying you to find out."

I closed my notebook and told him I'd get right on it. But I figured I'd better be honest with the man. You've got to have a bond of mutual trust with your client.

"I've got to warn you," I warned him, "I'm a pretty lousy detective, all things considered. I mean, I don't know if things like that matter to you, but I stink."

He said he knew that before he came up here. No decent detective would take a case like this.

He had already asked them. And they had already said no. So he had to take what he could get. He dug into his smelly pocket and pulled out his squalid checkbook. He tore off a check that had flies buzzing around it and handed it to me.

"I'm giving you a blank check."

"Why?"

"I don't have any money in the bank. But I will soon. Don't worry about the money. Just get going and solve this case. In fact, here are five more blank checks. That's how important this case is."

I agreed to take the case and tossed the blank checks in a drawer. I didn't have any other clients at the moment, and I didn't think my stomach could take another bodyguard job right now. Maybe this would turn into something.

Mandible left as regally as he had entered. I put on my hat, got my gun and notepad and headed for the door to see what kind of a start I could make on this case. My secretary watched me go, suspiciously.

"You're not going to be fooling around with any of those criminal women are you?" she asked.

I told her that wasn't too likely the way my day was going, but she would be the third to know.

CHAPTER THREE

Every detective has his own methods for solving a case, but for me it's mostly just legwork. When I first became a detective I had tried solving crimes the way mystery writers do: coming up with the solution to the crime first, then working back to the point where you don't know what the hell is going on. But for some reason every time I tried that I ended up locked in a closet. So now I just solve crimes the old fashioned way—I walk there.

The first person I went to see was a fence I knew named Frank. Frank the Fence, we used to call him. Then we'd laugh a little, because there were two "F"s in there. He never got the humor of it. It was easier to track him down than usual because instead of operating out of a dimly lit back room somewhere, or from a slowly moving automobile, he had a big neon sign over his downtown showroom that said "Frank's Fencing Service. We Pay Cash For Stolen Merchandise". That seemed a bit brazen to me, but I guessed that he knew what he was doing, and that the cops didn't.

I walked in, waited while Frank haggled with a bank robber over the value of a teller's window, then I asked Frank if he'd handled any worthless figurines lately. He asked me how stupid I thought he was. I told him and we stared at each other for awhile. Then he checked in the back.

"Just these," he said

He had a couple of Maltese Falcons, but that was about all. I thanked him for his time, reminded him that trafficking in stolen goods was illegal, wiped his spit from my eye, then went on my way.

Then I checked the pawnshops around town. Stolen merchandise often ends up in such places, despite the laws that discourage that. But the results I got were invariably disappointing. I would describe what I was looking for, they would listen, nod, then excitedly show me some second hand luggage and meerschaum pipes. I got the feeling they were more interested in making a sale than in helping me out. It's a sad commentary on something. Money money money, when will we ever learn?

During my visits to the pawnshops I noticed a lot of valuable merchandise was circulating around the city these days. A lot more than normal. Every shop seemed to be loaded with rare coins, old paintings, and all kinds of valuable collectibles. I asked the proprietors where all the good stuff came from and they got real excited and tried to sell me that luggage again, so I left. I don't want any luggage. I thought I had made that clear.

Even though Mandible had told me that his missing figurine had no intrinsic value, I thought I should check that out. So I went to several art galleries and showed the proprietors the picture Mandible had given me. They all made the same raspberry sound I had made, so that settled that.

I also made discrete inquiries about Mandible himself. It's important to know if your client has been telling you the whole truth. Because one of the things he's been telling you is that he's going to pay you. So I checked out his story. I got the same answer everywhere I went. People had seen Mandible around, but nobody could remember him ever being rich. He had always just seemed like a tramp to them.

I decided I'd better take a look at the house he said he had lived in. He said it was called Mandible Manor and was on top of the biggest hill in town. That should be easy to find, I thought confidently, even for a detective of my caliber. I got in my car and drove up there.

The gate didn't say Mandible Manor. It said Pellagra Place. And it looked like that name had been on the gate for a long time. I was familiar with the Pellagra crime family. Strictly minor leaguers, I had always thought. But that didn't fit with what I was seeing here.

I knocked on the door and asked to see the head of the house. The butler looked me over in that snooty way butlers have, put his gun away, and told me to wait. A few minutes later Big Al

Pellagra came to the door and asked what I wanted.

I told him what Mandible had told me. Pellagra frowned. He said he had never heard of a guy by that name and, more than that, he had never heard of me either. This guy had never heard of anybody. He said his family had always owned this place—everybody knew that—and I should get lost. I agreed I probably should. It would be best for everybody.

I went back to see Mandible at the address he had given me. It wasn't so much an address as a couple of cross streets. I found him sitting in a gutter, accosting passersby.

"Spare change, peasant? Oh it's you, Burly. Have you found out anything? Do you have a theory?"

"Yes, I'm working on the theory that you're a nut. I not only haven't found your figurine, I'm beginning to doubt there ever was one. I think that figurine of yours is one of those things people have in their minds, but it isn't anywhere else. And I've been checking around about you too. Nobody in town ever heard of you being anything but a tramp. Some added descriptive adjectives like 'stinky'."

Then I told him about my visit to "Mandible Manor", and how I'd discovered that it was actually named "Pellagra Place", and had been named that since it was built 60 years ago.

Mandible got pretty angry at this. "I specifically told you to confine your investigations to the figurine. You've exceeded your authority! Disobeyed instructions! Violated confidences!"

"Well I'm sorry."

"You'll be sorrier still if you disobey my instructions again. Now get back to work. And make sure you follow my orders to the letter this time."

"If it's all the same to you, I think I'll just resign from this case. I don't need your money that much, especially since it's so imaginary."

His tone changed immediately. "You can't quit. I need you. No one else will help me because I have no money to offer them and my story is so preposterous. You're my only chance. I need help. My family needs help."

He jerked a thumb back over his shoulder. I saw a group of snooty looking tramps eyeing me coldly.

"My daughter used to be the #6 ranked debutant in the city," he said. "She was fondled by Presidents. Now she counts herself lucky when she gets slobbered on by a garbage man. If you won't continue on this case for my sake, do it for hers."

I looked over at his daughter. She gave me the finger. I didn't really feel like doing anything for this family. I told Mandible so. He couldn't believe it. It was the most amazing thing he'd ever heard. The most astounding thing anyone had ever said. He couldn't believe he had heard me right. I told him he had. Now he couldn't believe that! This guy was making me tired.

"Thanks for the afternoon's entertainment," I

said. "I'll flush a copy of my bill down the toilet.
You should be getting it in a couple of days."

I left. Behind me I could hear the protesting
Mandible taking out his fury on a nearby dog turd.

I started heading for home. I had decided to
call this case "The Case Of The Lying Tramp".
Halfway down the street I spotted a small time
crook I knew named Small-Time Charlie. He was
walking down the street carrying a briefcase. I
wondered about this, because criminals do not
generally carry briefcases. It doesn't match the
rest of their costume. I wondered if this was some
new fad, like when criminals briefly went to the
see-through mask.

While I was watching him he looked around
to make sure no one was watching him, then
ducked into a telephone booth. It shimmered for
a second and went out of focus, then returned to
normal.

The door opened and Small-Time Charlie came
out. He was carrying a bag stuffed with money
and had a Van Gogh under his arm. He looked
around to make sure he still wasn't being
observed, then hurried down the street. This got
me curious. Small Time Charlie had gotten his
name from the small crimes he specialized in. A
big day for him was when he stole enough to stay
alive. He had started out stealing things from
people's garbage cans and then hiding them in
the dump. He stopped doing it when the city
started paying him for it. Seeing him making big
scores like this was intriguing to me. So I followed
him.

I kept about a block or so behind him all the way to the seedy hotel where he lived, gave him a couple minutes to drag the loot up to his room, then followed him up and knocked on the door.

"Nobody home," he called.

I thought about this. "Then who is talking to me?"

"The answering machine. Beat it, Burly."

The hinges on those old hotel doors are no match for the old Burly Shove. I forced open the door and ambled in.

"Hi, Charlie. I was in the neighborhood so I thought I'd drop by and nose around your home. See what I could find."

He was hanging up the Van Gogh next to a print of dogs cheating at cards.

"You can't just barge into people's happy hotel rooms like this. I got rights."

"I know. I just want to see what else you've got."

I gave the place the old Burly Onceover. It was obvious that Charlie had been doing very well since I saw him last. His cheap room was filled with valuable antiques and bales of cash. There were fancy paintings on the wall. I looked closer at one of them. It showed an old lady sitting in a chair.

"Did you paint this?" I asked. "Because it's good."

"Yeah, I painted it last night. So what? Get outta here. You ain't invited to as many places as you show up."

There was a brass plate attached to the frame that said "Whistler's Mother".

"Wait a minute," I said. "This is Whistler's Mother!"

"Used to be, maybe. It's my mother now."

Along with the paintings, there were also a number of diplomas on the walls from major universities issued in the name of "Professor Groggins", which Charlie informed me was his nom de college, the name he used when he graduated from colleges. It surprised me to find out that he was a learned man. I sat down on a small stack of gold bars and looked through some photo albums he had on a coffee table.

"These pictures of you?"

"Sure," he said. "Why? Don't they look like me?"

"Not really. They look more like an older, taller, different man."

He glanced at the pictures. "Those were taken back when I was different."

That didn't make sense, but it followed. I put the photo album down.

"Where'd you get all this money all of a sudden, Charlie? And if you've got so much money, why are you still living in this dump?"

"What do you mean? This is a great room. What's wrong with it? It's great." He looked around the room, suddenly not sure.

I kept questioning him for awhile, but I wasn't getting anywhere. He had an answer for everything, even if most of the answers were "none of your business, Burly" or "you already asked that, stupid." So I decided to cuff him around a little and see if that would shake any information loose. It's said that the first person who raises a hand in violence is the person who's run out of ideas. That's usually me. I run out of ideas fast. Violence I've got plenty of. While I was shaking him I threatened to call the police if I didn't get some answers that were more useful and less insulting to me personally.

"Go ahead and call them," he said. "I don't care. In fact, I'll call them myself."

He shook himself loose from my grasp, picked up the phone, and called the police. I confess this maneuver surprised me. I wasn't sure what my next move should be, so I pretended to look at some of the paintings on the walls, making what I hoped were intelligent sounding comments.

Five minutes later the cops arrived, listened to my story, then invited us both downtown to sort the matter out there, where they had better lighting and more ways to make people talk.

CHAPTER FOUR

Everything should have been great once we got to the police station. The police and I are on the same side in the fight for truth and justice. Teammates. Like ham and eggs. But I didn't like the way things were going this time. They had me in the interrogation room, where they were beating the stuffings out of me with their billy clubs. Meanwhile, Small-Time Charlie was behind the one-way glass watching me being interrogated and wearing an honorary police chief's hat.

"What do you want me to tell you?" I asked one of the cops.

"We want you to tell us how much this hurts."

They pounded me some more, then conferred. One of the cops said: "This is definitely the billy club for me, the Riot-King. I like the grip."

"I think I still prefer the Lump Master," said the second cop.

"Let me try that one again."

They beat me for a little longer, then tried out various truth serums on me. "Which truth serum tastes better?" asked one.

"It's hard to say," I said. "They're both so awful. This one, I guess."

"He's lying, Lieutenant."

They worked me over a little longer—trying out various brands of tear gas and suspect kicking boots on me—you can't beat that kind of "in the field" testing—then they spent a half hour pushing me off the tops of file cabinets. I don't know what that was about. I would have broken down and talked after awhile, but, like I said, they didn't seem to want to know anything. So I confined my comments to the occasional request that they quit it.

Finally they told me that Charlie had declined to press charges on the breaking and entering, so I was free to go. This was good news. I'm always glad to be free to go. But the way I'd been treated kind of stuck in my craw a little bit. There was part of a police pencil stuck in there too. As they were returning my possessions to me and processing me out, I took the opportunity to complain to the desk sergeant about the treatment I had received.

"The arresting officers didn't even read me my rights," I complained. "They just stapled them to my forehead."

The desk sergeant looked at me for a long moment. "That's awful," he said finally. "I blame myself."

Detecting a sympathetic ear, I started showing him some of my bruises. He made a slight motion with his head and two policemen walked up to me. I started showing them my bruises.

I picked myself up off the pavement in front of the police station and started limping home. I couldn't figure out why Charlie—clearly the bad guy here—had gotten such good treatment while I—the good man—had been knocked all over the lot. I also wondered where the police got all those valuable paintings they had on the walls. And where some of the policemen got those top hats they were wearing. The whole thing was a mystery to me. But then, most things are. I guess it's lucky for me I'm a detective.

As I was walking along puzzling about this, an elevator suddenly appeared on the street, I heard a small ding, the doors opened, and a bunch of crooks ran out of it at full speed carrying armloads of loot. Now there's something you don't see everyday, I thought. This, I felt, was something that should be looked into.

I walked over to the elevator and looked into it. There was nothing unusual about it at all. Just a perfectly ordinary elevator on a sidewalk. I scratched my head. Scratching my head made pieces of it come off and reminded me that I needed some bandages for about 90% of my body. So I resumed walking home. I'd come back and look into the elevator mystery again later.

I turned the corner and headed up a residential street, bumping into a half-knocked-down mailbox. I straightened it. Then I noticed the name on the mailbox: Professor Groggins. That name rang a bell. I looked up at the house. The door was wide open and hanging on one hinge. The front window was broken, and there was a trail of valuables leading from the porch to the sidewalk. Looked like trouble at the old Groggins place. I headed into the house to take a look.

It was obvious that Professor Groggins' house had been robbed very thoroughly. There were even empty spaces on the wall where it looked like some diplomas had been hanging. I remembered the diplomas on Small-Time Charlie's wall. There was some connection there. I'd figure out what it was in a minute. I found the door to the basement and went down to see if anything was missing down there.

The basement was set up as some kind of a laboratory. It had been tossed pretty good too. All that was left were a lot of half finished inventions. It began to dawn on me that this guy Groggins must be an inventor.

I could see why the burglars would have left all these gadgets behind. Pawnshops and fences weren't interested in unfinished merchandise, no matter what their scientific importance—they'd been burned by Einstein and his crowd before—so there was no easy way to turn these things into cash. But one invention had definitely been stolen from the room. A glass case had been smashed open and the contents had been removed. Above the case was a sign that said "Time Machine - Mark V".

Mandible was still living in the gutter when I got there, but now he had a tramp butler. So I guess things were looking up for him. The butler stepped in front of me and asked me my business. I told him I came to see Mandible.

"I'll see if he's in, sir," said the butler.

"I can see him sitting in the sewer."

"I will see if he's in sir," repeated the butler firmly.

The butler announced me to Mandible, who waved regally for me to approach him. He was using a couple of stray dogs as a table, and had his feet up on some crud. I sloshed over into his august presence and told him he might not be so crazy after all.

He snorted. "Tell me something I don't know."

"All right. I'm not sure if it has anything to do with the loss of your figurine, but the criminals in this town seem to have a time machine."

"What!"

I recounted to him some of the strange things I'd seen lately and what I'd found at Professor Groggins' house.

"So that's how it was done! Of course!" He gave me a look. "I see you're finally beginning to believe my story."

"Maybe some of it", I said. "I don't know. I still don't want your autograph yet."

"But you're back on the case? Good. Now I want you to find that time machine, get hold of it somehow, then report back to me for further instructions. Here's another blank check."

He absently reached into his pocket, pulled out a piece of paper and handed it to me. I looked at it. It was a fast food wrapper. It was probably as valuable as anything else he'd given me, so I stuck it in my wallet. As I walked away I looked back and saw that Mandible seemed to be doing his best to rebuild his fortune, using what he had at hand.

"Turds for sale!" he shouted. "I've got turds!"

CHAPTER FIVE

Since I didn't know what the time machine looked like, or where it might be, the first thing I did was check out a few places I wanted to go anyway; the ball game, the movie theater, I went ice skating. Then, acting on a hunch, I bought a new suit. It all goes on the old expense account. I mean, all the time I'm doing these other things, I'm thinking about your important case. However, I made a mental note not to overdo this sort of thing or next year I might be reclassified as a crook. I'm always making mental notes like that. You've got to keep improving yourself or you'll go nuts.

I went down to Broadway & 4th to talk to the underworld characters who normally hang around there socializing with each other between crimes, practicing the various skills necessary to being a successful criminal; picking each other's pockets, playing dumb at each other, and so on, and betting with each other who can talk the most like a Damon Runyon character.

I leaned up against a wall next to one of them

and chewed a toothpick as he was doing until I felt we had formed a loose bond. Then I said: "How's the life of crime going?"

"Not too good," he said. "I been under the weather. I missed a bank robbery last week. Had to call in sick. The bank president didn't know what I was talking about. I think it's the climate that gets me. How are you?"

"Okay." I chewed my toothpick for a thoughtful moment. "I've got a ten-spot here needs a home."

"You interest me strangely. What are you asking for in exchange?"

"Information about a time machine."

His face suddenly got wooden. He looked away from me and spoke in a stilted manner. "I - do - not - know - what - you - mean - sir."

I tried again, saying the same thing using different words, spoken at different volume levels, but he didn't bite. Finally I turned to another crook.

"Let's play word games! How about 'Word Association'? I'll go first: TIME MACHINE!!! THEFT OF!!!"

He didn't want to play. In fact, none of the crooks were interested in talking about time machines. The more I talked about time machines, the more they left. The last one to go was carrying a briefcase that said "Prof. E. Groggins" on the side.

"Professor Groggins? I asked.

"Yes?"

"There seems to be a lot of people in this town with that name."

"Yes. We had quite a laugh about that, me and them."

He followed the others, and I was alone with as many unanswered questions as I had had before.

I decided to talk to Handicap Harry, who had been known to have information for sale from time to time. That's not his real name, of course. Good parents don't give their kids gangster names anymore. Handicap Harry is more of a nickname the other guys in his social set gave him. And not because he liked to bet on the ponies, but because he had a wooden leg, a hook for a hand, a toupee, a glass chest, and all sorts of other replacement parts. He'd had a tough life, I guess.

He didn't answer my knock so I put my shoulder to the door, gave it my trademark Burly Shove, and walked in. Harry was on the bed, just a bald head on a pillow, with all the rest of him carefully stowed around the room.

"Get outta here," he said.

"I just wanted to ask you some questions, Harry. Then you can ask me some. There are probably all sorts of things you'd like to know about me. We can take turns. Back and forth, kind of fair like. I'll get the ball rolling by asking you about time machines. Then you can ask me something. Then more time machine questions."

"I said get outta here. Or I'll bite your brains out."

Well I didn't want that to happen, that would be awful, so I left. But I was a little peeved that he wasn't more civil to such a welcome guest as me so, and maybe I shouldn't have done it, I put my mouth to the keyhole and yelled "Fire!", trying to give the impression that the building was burning. I could hear consternation and thrashing around inside, then I heard a head roll off the bed and thump on the floor. Like I said, I probably shouldn't have done that.

Then I tried something I always try at least once in the course of an investigation. I put on a ten gallon hat and adopted the persona of my alter-ego Billy Bob Burly, a loudmouthed Texas oilman, and tried to con some useful information out of a crook I saw hanging around outside a cigar store.

Like always, my impersonation wasn't perfect. My accent kept slipping from Texan to Swedish, and my cowboy hat kept falling off. But I kept plugging away. You've got to give the scam a chance to work. But I wasn't conning much information out of this particular mark. In fact he wasn't saying anything. He was just looking at me like I was a train wreck. Pretty soon, as usual, I was forgetting my lines and having to start over, until I finally just tore up my script, jumped up and down on my cowboy hat and sat down on the curb to brood, telling the mark to get away from me or I would shoot him.

Now I've seen detectives on TV work that same con with 100% success. It works every time for them. I've tried to talk to statisticians about my unbelievable 0% success rate—I mean what are the odds of that?—but they say they're not interested. Even though it's their specialty! That's what's wrong with America today, I guess. Something like that. I know something's wrong with America. Maybe that's it.

Next I tried a good old-fashioned stakeout. I like these because they're easy. You're not trying to outwit anybody. In fact you're not trying to do anything. You're just sitting quietly and comfortably for hours at a time waiting for some other poor slob to do something. I'm great at that. And all the time you're sitting there you get to quietly listen to your car radio, and eat all kinds of stuff: donuts, salted snacks, you name it. Anything goes on a stakeout. I didn't know what to watch for exactly in this stakeout, so I just parked where I had a good vantage point of things in general. When I couldn't see out of my car anymore because of all the parking tickets that had been slapped on my windshield, I figured it was time to call it a day. It was another failure, intelligence-wise, but like I said, I like stakeouts.

On the way back to the office I stopped and questioned a burglar who I happened to see robbing a house.

After a half dozen questions, the burglar became impatient. "Hey look, Burly, if you're going to keep asking me questions, at least give me a hand with some of these bulkier items."

I helped him carry a stereo out to his getaway car and tie up and gag the homeowner, while I questioned him some more. He said he didn't know anything about any time machine. He said I should ask H.G. Wells. I wrote down the name.

By the time I got back to my office, I was dog

tired. I'd put in a long day and found nothing. I asked my secretary if she'd seen either a figurine or a time machine lately. You never know. It doesn't hurt to ask. Maybe she was sitting on them or something.

"Just get away from me," she said. "You make me sick."

Normally, I wouldn't let an employee talk to me like that. But she's quit so many times neither one of us remembers whether she's working for me right now or not. Since I wasn't sure of her current status, I changed the subject by asking her why I couldn't get into the office this morning. Where was she at 11 am?

She bristled. "Look, do you want me to show up on time, or do you want me to do my job right?"

"Either one, I guess. I'll take what I can get at this point."

"Stop shouting at me. My ear hurts. I'm going home."

I guess I should treat my employees better. If she is an employee.

CHAPTER SIX

That evening an elite group of the city's most influential criminals met to decide what to do about me. I'd been asking too many questions, they felt, and not giving them enough time to think of witty answers before moving on to the next question.

After various solutions to the so-called "Burly Problem" had been advanced, they finally decided to just try warning me off the case first. It would be the simplest, cheapest way. The organization's ammo bill last year was through the roof. Things had gotten so bad that they had to let some pickpockets and rapists go just before Christmas. So, since threats are cheaper than bullets, they decided to go that way.

Not long after this decision was made, my doorbell rang. I went to the door and opened it. Two men were standing there. One was pointing a gun at me.

"Oh no!" I said.

The guy with the gun sneered at me. "Aren't you glad to see us?"

"Of course not."

The criminals came into my apartment. One was very tall, the other was very small. Actually, they were both about average height. I was using artistic license there. I'm told this is the thing to do, as it makes the story more interesting. If one guy is the size of a refrigerator and the other one is the size of a thumbtack, this conjures up a vivid picture in the mind. It's like you can see the one guy being smaller than the other, and this interests you. Readers get bored if everybody's the same size. Anyway, these two guys came into the room in their various sizes and looked around. I hadn't expected visitors, so the room wasn't looking its best.

The smaller crook said: "Geez, what kind of guy would live like this? It's like a pig lives here."

I frowned. "I'm already mad about you breaking in and pointing a gun at me. Don't make it worse."

The smaller crook covered his mouth with his handkerchief. "I gotta get out of here, Boss. The dust and the mold is getting to me."

"Have you taken your medicine?

"Yes, but it's not helping."

The guy with the gun turned to me. "I'll have to make this short. We just stopped in to give you some friendly advice, Burly. There are some things going on around town right now that don't concern you, things involving time machines and other advanced scientific concepts understood by few. Our friendly advice to you is that you keep your nose out of these things, or you and your nose are dead men."

When guys get tough with me like that, I usually try to make some kind of tough sounding wisecrack, but tough sounding wisecracks aren't as easy to think up as you would think. I mean, if I was good at wisecracks, I'd be working for Milton Berle, not you.

They waited for a few minutes for me to come up with a wisecrack, while I just stood there thinking and staring and sweating, then they left. I would have thought of one.

I had another group of unexpected visitors the following morning. They were in my office waiting for me when I arrived. Detective Sgt. Dodge and his merry men from the 4th Precinct.

My secretary, Elizabeth, looked at me accusingly. "What have you done now?"

"I don't know."

"If they want me to testify against you, I'll do it."

"You are a gem," I said.

I wasn't particularly happy to see Sgt. Dodge. No one ever was. He had a disconcerting habit of pinching your face between his thumb and forefinger when he was talking to you, so he could be sure you were paying attention to him. I didn't like that approach. Nobody did. Not even the Mayor.

I walked over to Dodge and asked him to what I owed the extreme pleasure?

"Just a friendly warning from your friendly local police department," he said. "The friendly warning reads as follows: Dear Friend. If you continue your current investigations, we of the police cannot guarantee your personal safety."

"What's different about that?" I asked.

"I didn't say it was different. I just said to watch out."

"I see. Well, thanks."

He let go of my face, pocketed a couple of items that caught his fancy and left. This was two friendly warnings I had received in one 24 hour time period. A personal best. But friendly warnings aren't always as friendly as they sound. That night I wrote the word "yikes" in my diary.

Nonetheless, I went back on the streets to continue my investigations. It might seem stupid to you that I did this, but probably my whole job seems stupid to you. What it comes down to is the only way I know how to make a living in the detective business is to be tenacious, tough, and something else that begins with T. The three T's. If I let people scare me off a case, word would get around and they'd scare me off all my cases. Then they'd probably scare me out of town. Maybe all the way to Germany. I couldn't let them scare me that far away. It wouldn't be good business.

That evening I checked out a nightclub that was known to be frequented by criminal types, and was in fact run by criminals. It wasn't the most pleasant place to spend an evening; the food and drinks were terrible, and the entertainment wasn't much better. I guess it's hard to find criminals who have really mastered big band instruments. But it was a place an investigator like myself could pick up some leads. I hung around the bar, listening to the various furtive conversations that were going on around me. A couple of guys near me were planning a big heist, apparently. After awhile, they noticed I was listening in, partly because I kept asking them to repeat things. I've got to quit doing that. That's a real tipoff.

One of the crooks finally glared at me. "Do you mind? We're trying to have a private conversation."

"Not at all," I said. I moved away, but then leaned back in so my ear was actually a little closer to them than it was before. Then I made the ear widen a little. They probably wouldn't have noticed, except I lost my balance a little bit there and my ear went into one of their drinks. They picked up what was left of their drinks and went off to a table in the corner. I didn't bother waiting for them to invite me to join them. I wasn't picking up any information here anyway.

The next day, a dead turtle was left on my doorstep as a warning. I couldn't figure out as a warning for what, and I guess whoever was watching me picked up on that, because the next morning there was another dead turtle, but this one had several sheets of paper glued to it's back leg. The pieces of paper contained a long footnoted explanation of all the symbolism involved. It didn't make a lot of sense to me. The turtle was the "turtle of inquisitiveness" and the cheese smeared on it's shell meant something, and the little cowboy boots on its feet meant something.

Everything about this animal meant something apparently to whoever sent it. I still didn't get what it was all about. The next morning there was no turtle. Somebody just shot at me from the bushes.

The fact that I had continued my investigations despite their friendly warnings, delivered by them in what they felt was a friendly way, amazed the crooks and, yes, it kind of hurt their feelings too. This was not the way friends acted, they felt. It prompted a late-night visit to my home of four thugs, who invited me to come along with them for a little ride.

While this invitation was being delivered, the leader of the group absently picked lint off my shoulder and eyelashes off my eyelids. This helped me come to my decision. I would go along with them. I said a well lighted area might be a fun place to go, maybe someplace with a lot of witnesses, but they said they would choose the destination.

They took me to a drive-in movie. About half way in to the second feature, they told me what was on their minds. They didn't want me nosing around asking about TIME MACHINES ever again. They felt they had made themselves clear on this before, but obviously some facets of the matter had remained vague. They wanted to take this opportunity to make their request louder and clearer. They attached a drive-in speaker to each of my ears, then, tying into the theater's sound system, repeated their warning at such a volume that, as I write this, my head is still vibrating enough to seem to be playing a little song. Then they asked politely if I had heard them this time. I said I sure did, boy. Heard it that time. Loud and clear. They said good.

As they drove me home, they told me a story about another man who hadn't paid attention to their warnings. What was left of him was found by some Russians who were walking in space. If this story was true, it was alarming. I asked if it was true. They said it was. This was alarming.

CHAPTER SEVEN

I continued my investigations the next day, but more warily now, disguising myself by starting to grow a mustache. Surprisingly, this didn't help. It's like they didn't look at my upper lip at all.

I was outside a movie theater studying the marquee which said "The Time Machine" and wondering if this was a clue, when some tough boys came around the corner and started heading my way, fitting brass knuckledusters onto their hands. This didn't look like just a warning. This looked like something more painful than that. Maybe we were past the warning stage. I tried to lose them by taking off at full speed down the street, suddenly spinning around and then racing past them the other way. I found out that doesn't work when you're on foot. You need a car for that. They just grabbed me by the neck as I went by.

I said: "Look, if you're going to hit me try to hit me in the middle part of my head. The front and back already hurt like hell. And try to leave a mark. My insurance company doesn't believe me half the time."

I'm not sure they were even listening to my instructions. They rebuked me for continuing on the case when I had been asked so nicely not to, and expressed scorn for the flimsy disguise I was attempting to grow. Then they pounded me to a pulp and dumped me in the middle of a roller rink, with my butt sticking way up in the air. So there's the embarrassment factor too.

Recovering from the beating at home, I looked at myself in the mirror. It was me all right. Still me. Good old me. My clothes were pretty torn up though. People don't realize that when a detective gets beaten up his shirt and pants take a licking too, and clothing isn't cheap these days. Ask anybody. And clothing stores don't take trade-ins, so it can run into some money. Ask those same guys from before.

The next morning a knocking woke me up. It was somebody knocking my head against a pipe. It was those same tough boys from the day before. They said they were on their way back from killing a milkman and had decided to stop by to see if I remembered what we had all discussed yesterday. I said sure. Was I going to be looking for any time machines today? I said sure. I tend to not know what people are asking me when I just wake up, so I usually just say sure.

They beat me up again, just as badly as the day before, but they weren't allowed into the roller rink with me this time. The management had had enough. So they just dumped me in the dump.

I went to the cops to complain about all the rough stuff. Sgt. Dodge was philosophical about it. "Well, that's what happens," he said.

"I know it's what happens. I want you to do something about it. That's usually what happens next."

He said the police were a little busy right now, trying to think up ways to harass private detectives who couldn't keep their noses out of things which weren't any of their business. Could I come back later? I said I could. He let go of my face and I left.

The lights were red for me all the way back to the office, for some reason, and there didn't seem to be a way to turn onto my street anymore. I finally had to get out of my car and walk. When I got to my building, I discovered that the sidewalks around it were all being repaired at the same time, so I had a hard time getting up to my office. I had to jump through my window from another building.

When I got into my office, I found that it had been vandalized. Tables were overturned, papers were scattered around the room, and the words "You Asked For It" were spray painted on the walls. I figured some crooks must have done it, at first. Or maybe the cops. I seemed to have a lot of enemies these days. Then I found out from my secretary that it was done by that cut-rate interior decorator I had hired. I called him up and told him "this is not what we discussed. It's kind of like what we discussed, but not exactly". Then I hung up. Never again. From now on I'm going to pay top dollar for interior decoration.

The next day I got word that my private investigator's license had been suspended, and my address had been revoked. Some guys from the city came over and scraped the numbers off my house. I wondered if this would affect my mail deliveries.

All of this was making me start to rethink my whole approach to crime detection. Maybe being tenacious wasn't such a valuable weapon in my arsenal after all. Lately it had been causing me more trouble than it was worth. I thought of maybe dropping it from the 3 T's. Maybe go to 2 T's.

That night I was having a drink at a bar, thinking over the whole "T" thing, and taking the opportunity to quiz the other patrons about time machines—I tried to make a game of it—see who could divulge the most information in 60 seconds—when a criminal type at a nearby table offered to buy me a drink.

I thanked him and said I'd take some 80 year old champagne, if he and his henchmen would join me. He said that was fine. Instead of calling the waiter, he reached into his pocket and poured a can of something into a champagne glass and handed it to me. I noticed none of my companions were drinking. I asked about this. They said they would drink theirs after I drank mine. Some custom of theirs, presumably.

The whole thing seemed a little suspicious— when you've been in the business as long as I have you start to get suspicious—so I didn't gulp the drink right down like I usually do with liquor I don't have to pay for. I sipped it kind of slow-like. It tasted okay, and I couldn't see any indication that I was being drugged. Everyone in the bar looked like kangaroos just like they should, so, reassured, I gulped the rest down and yelled for another.

The next few days are kind of a blur to me. I don't remember much of what happened. I kept a diary, but my entries for those days just say "Ha ha ha ha hahhhh hah ha."

When I finally came out of it, I found that I was in a locked room with barred windows in one of our city's more crooked and unpleasant private sanitariums. It didn't look good for old Burly, I thought. Ha ha hahhh ha!

The door to my room was almost never opened. My food was slid under the door, giving all my meals a similar thickness and appearance. And I was expected to go to the bathroom under this same door. The guy who designed that place should have been shot.

They kept me in a half-conscious state most of the time. Drugged enough so I wouldn't cause them any trouble, but conscious enough so that when they beat me I was capable of giving out a real good yell. I held up under all this pretty well. I was sleeping like a baby—waking up every three hours screaming and crapping my pants.

The only time escape was a possibility was when the doctor came in twice a week to administer additional drugs to me and slap me around a little. I hoped I might get a chance to overpower him, but he had a lot of experience in places like this and didn't even let me get close to him. He administered the drugs using a nine foot needle, and slapped me with a glove on a pole.

But one week the regular doctor didn't show up—I think I heard he was skiing in Nazi Germany—and there was a substitute doctor doing his rounds. I informed this substitute that not only were his shoes seriously untied but there was something completely on his back. While he was tying himself into knots addressing these problems, I hit him over the head with my bed.

A few minutes later I was in the corridor, dressed as a doctor. All I had to do now was talk my way past the guard and I was home free. Despite my optimism, I shouldn't have been able to convince the guard that I was one of the staff doctors, because I was still heavily drugged and my smock was on backwards and I was drooling and one eye wouldn't stay open. I certainly didn't look like a very stylish doctor.

But I did manage to talk my way out because the guy I was talking to, a dazed drooling guard, with his uniform only partially covering his institutional pajamas, was also trying to talk his way out.

So we both got out together and ran like hell in all directions, both of us ending up in the same getaway car, with me driving and him yelling to turn left.

I was back to normal physically in a day or two, but I was still angry for another week. Once I had recovered, I decided to go see Mandible and talk to him about maybe upping my daily rate a little. This case was dangerous. Only additional money would fix that. I headed downtown in my car.

I never got there. Somebody had been doing some major league tampering to my car. The brake lines were cut. The tires were on fire. There was carbon monoxide coming out of everything. And the radio was tuned to a station I didn't like. I had to tip my booby-trapped hat to whoever tampered with this car.

I was late with my payments on the car anyway, and it looked like a lot of repair work was going to have to be done no matter how this came out, so I figured let the finance company worry about it. I called them up on my cell phone, told them where the car was, and jumped out.

I was going over sixty at the time, but luckily I didn't hit the ground. There was a cliff there and I just went harmlessly over that. But just when you're sailing along, thinking everything is going to be okay, something unexpected comes along to jar you out of your complacency. For me, in this case, it was the bottom of the cliff. I got bruised up pretty bad—they say I bounced for an hour—but luckily no bones were broken. That's where that protective layer of fat I was telling you about comes in.

After word got out that I had escaped from their clutches and defied death yet again, the criminals held another emergency meeting. Apparently I was too tough and stupid to be stopped by normal means. Tough and stupid is a hard combination to beat, say the experts. So they decided to try another tack. Maybe beauty would tame the beast. They would get the irresistible vamp, Cola, to lure me to my doom.

CHAPTER EIGHT

Cola was reclining on silken cushions, getting a quick touchup from her makeup team, and last minute instructions from her trainer, when I arrived carrying a bunch of roses and a box of candy.

I hadn't realized I was so handsome before this, but according to this woman, if I heard her properly, I was a combination of Gregory Peck. She said she had to have a date with me right away. Tonight. And she told me to come alone. No cops. Apparently she felt if policemen were there it would be hard for us to get comfortable.

Cola took the roses and candy I had brought her and daintily chucked them onto a huge pile of roses and candy in the corner. She folded me in her arms and said she couldn't live without me, which was confusing because she'd been living without me for about thirty six years, by my estimate, judging by her teeth. (I forced open her jaws while she was putting on some music.)

We sat down on the couch. She held me close and whispered in my ear how wonderful I was.

Since I'm not wonderful, I was pretty sure this was a trap. So I figured I'd better grope her as much as I could before they sprung the trap. You've got to take what you can get in this life. I read that in a magazine. So I started smearing kisses on her and pawing the front of her dress, trying to get my money's worth before somebody bashed my head in.

She kept moaning "Frank!... Frank!..." and I kept asking "What?... what?..." Suddenly she pulled away.

"What's wrong?" I asked.

"I can't do it. I was supposed to pepper you with kisses and then knock you on the head with a champagne bucket, but..."

"But your better nature prevailed?"

"No, you're just so unattractive to me. I don't care if our whole plan falls through. I'm not going to do it."

I tried to be helpful. "Maybe if you thought of someone else?"

She shook her head. "I've thought of everybody else. Nothing works."

I was disappointed that our date was going to be over so soon. For this I got my hair cut, I thought. But at least I hadn't fallen into any kind of trap. At that moment, out of the corner of my eye, I saw a dark shape rushing towards me. Then fifty more shapes. Then more fists than you could count, more fists than there are in the rainbow, started punching the bejesus out of me.

When I woke up I was being dragged by my feet down a long cement corridor, through metal doors, then down more corridors, always winding farther down under the street. It's embarrassing being dragged like that. And yes, it scrapes your head up pretty good too. So that makes two things wrong with it. It wasn't the best situation to find yourself in, of an evening, but I tried to stay upbeat and make the best of it. I sang a few songs, made plans for what I was going to do tomorrow, if there was a tomorrow, waved to the armed guards in the corridor etc.

I asked one of the armed guards if he could help me out. I said there was some guy dragging me by the feet. That guy with the crew cut. I suggested that there might be a few bucks in it for him if he would join the Burly Team. He didn't answer. Probably thinking about something else.

I was dragged into a big room which, I was told used to be part of our city's Civil Defense system, but was now owned by the Pellagra Crime Family. The city's rationale for selling their Civil Defense System was that it would save taxpayers x amount of dollars a year—they never got more specific than that—and was no longer needed. Though they admitted that in the unlikely event of a nuclear attack, the public would probably have to go screw themselves, they stressed that this was a worse case scenario.

The big room I was in was the command center, which had all sorts of viewer screens and consoles and scary looking launch buttons, so you could conduct an entire nuclear war from in there if you wanted to. Pretty slick, I thought. Wish I had one of these.

The crook who had been dragging me said they had gotten tired of trying to kill me. It was too hard, for some reason. They didn't know why. I started telling him about my protective layer of fat, but he told me to shutup. He said they'd run out of ideas, so they just decided to just toss me down here.

"Why don't you kill me now? While I'm upside down?" I asked. I like pointing out to criminals when they're being inconsistent or their reasoning has some stupid flaw. But he just gave me a look that seemed to say I should mind my own business. Then he actually said I should mind my own business. So that's what that look meant, all right.

He told me the crooks used this place for more than just a dumping ground for undesirables. He said they also had a lot of food stored here in case there was ever a nuclear war. That way they could insure that in the future there would still be criminals.

He said they even had a selective breeding program going on down here, trying to breed the perfect criminal by crossing themselves with gorgeous showgirls. I asked how the gorgeous showgirl part helps make the criminal.

"Wouldn't it be better to have the women be scrawny and beady-eyed?" I ventured. "Maybe with the face of a rat?"

"Hey, you have your selective breeding program, we'll have ours."

While he was untying my hands, straightening my jacket and combing my hair, I pointed out that this is where the bad guys always make their big mistake, giving the good guy, that's me in this instance, all the information he needs to destroy them, letting him in on all their most criminal secrets.

"When I escape from your clutches, you're screwed," I told him.

I waited for him to blab some secrets to me, but he just left and slammed the door. So I figured now probably wasn't the time. He'd tell me later, most likely. And then he would be screwed. I looked around. I wasn't alone.

There were about two dozen other prisoners in the huge room. They were looking at me curiously, but also trying to cover as much of the floor with their bodies as they could so as to lay claim to that much space. Among them I recognized a couple of honest politicians and several honest cops I'd seen around who were plainly regretting their choice of sides by now.

Then I saw a geeky old guy with glasses, wearing a smock that had "Professor Groggins" embroidered above the pocket. I was getting sick of everybody I met being named Professor Groggins, but something told me this was the real Professor Groggins. And that something was him.

CHAPTER NINE

"**I** am the real Professor Groggins," he said.

I made him show me three pieces of I.D. before I would let him say anything more. Then I asked him what he was doing here.

He told me that the crooks had broken into his home during a routine burglary, and had stolen everything from his lab that had looked like it was valuable, including the time machine he had invented. After they had found out the time machine really worked, they came back and stole Groggins himself so he could invent more useful devices for them.

"They've kept me here for who knows how long..."

"Two weeks," I said.

"I've completely lost track of time."

"Two weeks."

"Bush was president when they put me in here."

"Two weeks ago."

He complained about the treatment he'd received since he had arrived, especially the

Sunday Brunch, which he felt was uninspired, and all the evil laughing in this place was keeping him awake at night. He probably would have kept complaining indefinitely, but I reminded him that I didn't work there, and if I did work there I probably wouldn't be working in the Complaints Department. I'd more likely have some kind of lifting job.

I asked him what he had invented for them so far. He said nothing had been completed yet, but they had him working on a machine that fixes horse races so the dishonest horse wins every time, a machine that makes their enemies nine feet tall, so they can see them coming, and a milk-shake machine. "I just bought them one of those," he said.

Then Groggins told me about the time machine; what it looked like, how it worked, and so on. After 35 or 36 hours of explanation I figured I understood what the thing was. "A briefcase," I said.

"Yes."

I won't bore you with the technical aspects of the machine, because, like me, you're probably too stupid to understand most of it. You're good looking though. Damn good looking. Don't forget that. But basically the way it worked was this: the time mechanism itself was contained in an ordinary businessman's briefcase. All you had to do was open the briefcase, turn the machine on, fast forward past the welcoming messages and the advertisements for other of Groggins' inventions, set the dials for the year you wanted to travel to, then wait to be blasted into the void.

When the machine made a connection with another time period, a five foot square opening opened up in both the current time period and the period you were going to. This hole closed back up when your journey was complete. While the hole was open, people in both time periods could look in and see what was going on in the other time period and shout abuse at each other. "1958 Sucks! 1743 Rules!", that sort of thing.

Only the briefcase was needed to travel through this hole, but Groggins said you should always remember to duck into a phone booth, or an elevator or some other small walled-in space before turning on the machine.

"You want to be in an enclosed space when you travel through time. Otherwise you'll be hit by rocks, bottles and other debris," he said.

"Why?"

"Oh, I don't know. It's a jealousy thing probably, resentment. Who knows why people throw things?"

I more or less understood the science of the thing now, but I still couldn't figure out what crooks would want with a time machine. What would they use it for? Historical research? That seemed pretty unlikely to me. Don't make me laugh. I mean, who are they trying to fool? This is bullshit. Groggins explained that if you're a criminal, having mastery over time is very useful in a number of ways.

"It's good for extremely quick getaways, for

example," he said. "One second after committing a crime you can be 1000 miles and 4 years away. And it can help you establish a terrific alibi. You can rob a bank in broad daylight, writing your name all over all the people you've just robbed, then prove conclusively that you were in five other places when the robbery occurred. No one with an alibi like that has ever been convicted in the United States. You can also go back in time and steal things and then return to the present with no danger of being prosecuted. Because the statute of limitations will have run out on the crime. I understand they've already stripped 1995 of every penny it had. And you can go back in time and win bar bets from people in the past who don't know, for example, that Lincoln is about to be assassinated. That's why Lincoln died broke. His estate had to pay out millions to gamblers. It was his own fault. He should have smelled something fishy with all those bets going down on Friday April 14th. He should have laid some of the bets off."

After hearing all this I agreed that a time machine could be very useful to a criminal. I also agreed that Lincoln should have stuck to politics.

Then I suggested Groggins must be pretty upset that the criminals were using his wonderful machine for evil purposes. He said not really. Some of the things he'd planned on using it for were kind of evil too. What irritated him was that they weren't being more careful with it. They left it in cloakrooms, in the back seats of taxicabs, tossed it in dumpsters, and so on. Sheer carelessness. Sometimes it would be days before it turned up in some lost and found somewhere. They had no respect for the machine at all.

"And they exercise no care when they're time traveling," he said. "They could inadvertently cause all sorts of time paradoxes and incongruities in the space/time continuum."

"That's what I was thinking."

He went on and on about how delicate space and time was, but frankly I didn't buy it. I mean, if you think it's so easy to change the course of world events, try it. You don't need a time machine. You're already living in somebody's past and somebody else's future. Just step on a bug or something and see what that gets you. See if now you were never born, or suddenly now there's fifty Hitlers in your bathroom, crapping all over everything. It ain't going to happen. Anyway, that's what I figured.

Now that I knew what the time machine looked like, all I had to do was escape and find it. Then I could probably take the rest of the day off.

CHAPTER TEN

It was harder to break out of that place than I thought it would be. Now I know how nuclear bombs feel. Those walls are thick. Damn thick. The old Burly Shove didn't work at all. Neither did the Burly Nose Ram. So I decided to get tricky.

First I tried going through the ventilation duct, but I just ended up inside a huge air conditioner. I'm told they could hear my screams all over the building, coming out of all those little vents, and that many people in the building found this annoying. A number of them had to turn their TVs up. I try to keep it down in situations like that, but sometimes you just can't.

Then I convinced all the other prisoners to help me build a big fire, explaining that we would all be able to escape when the criminals smelled the smoke, panicked, and opened the door. I forgot how airtight those Civil Defense places are. Nobody smelled any smoke except us. And we smelled it too well.

The other prisoners didn't have anything else to put out the fire with, so they used me. Then

61

they stubbed me out and tossed me in the corner. That's what you get for trying to be a leader. Sometimes I don't know why we leaders bother.

By this time I was pretty much out of escape ideas. That's the way it usually is with me. Once I've climbed into something and set fire to something else, I'm done. I always read about people in these situations suddenly saying "I've got a plan". And they do! And it's great! Where do they get all these plans, that's what I want to know. I never have any plans. And why didn't they think of a plan before, so they wouldn't be in this fix? I don't get it.

I checked with Groggins to see if he could think of anything. Maybe he was one of those guys with all the plans. To my amazement, he not only had a plan, he already had an escape device built. I was impressed. This was just outstanding.

The crooks had set up a small lab down there for Groggins to work on inventions for them. In his spare time he had been secretly working on an escape device for himself. It was a teleporting machine like they have in Star Trek. In fact, he said he got the idea and the design by watching an episode of Star Trek. He said he did most of his research in this way—by reading science fiction books and watching monster movies, and so on. I looked at him like he was nuts. He noticed the look and immediately got defensive.

"I realize my methods are unconventional. Some people think I'm mad. But you don't, do you?"

"Sure."

He felt I might not be looking at the thing from the right angle. "I might just be ahead of my time. People often mistake genius for insanity. That might be what's happening here."

"You're the screwiest guy I've ever met."

He decided I didn't fully understand how his technique worked. That was the problem. He took a moment to explain.

"All the real worthwhile inventions have already been thought of by hack science fiction writers," he informed me. "I'm surprised no one has actually sat down and tried to build any of the stuff they write about. A lot of it is really easy to make. Disintegrating rays, invisibility potions, time machines; the hard thing isn't developing these inventions, it's coming up with the concept in the first place. The hack writers of the world are the real geniuses. But they're bad businessmen. They think up the idea, figure out how the machine would have to work, then sell the whole concept to whoever wants it for a few dollars. Plus they give you an exciting story too. All the inventor has to do is experiment around to find the missing pieces of the puzzle. And if you steal one of their ideas and make a fortune off it they're completely happy and swagger around saying they "forsaw it". If they're satisfied with that, fine. I wouldn't be. I'd be suing everybody's asses off."

He said he got the time machine right on the fifth try. The first four didn't so much travel in time as they burned down his house. But he said this first version of his teleporter looked to him like a winner.

Against my better judgment, I let him talk me into sitting down in his teleporter and giving it a try. But aside from scorching my clothes and blowing off some of my hair, it didn't do anything. He said no problem. He told me to go get some coffee and read a magazine over and over. He'd have his Teleporter Mark II finished in less than a year.

I didn't want to wait that long so I quit being cute about the whole thing and just launched myself out of a missile silo.

I'm not very ballistically shaped, so I only flew about eighty yards before I landed on top of a restaurant.

As I limped home, I saw a long line of criminals impatiently waiting their turn to get into a photo booth. That seemed odd to me. Criminals are vain, but not that vain. At the most they get their pictures taken maybe once a month. And usually they have it done at the police station where it's free. While I was puzzling about this, the booth shimmered and went out of focus briefly, then the door opened and a crook came out carrying some loot and a briefcase. He handed the briefcase to the next crook, who went inside and the booth started shimmering and going out of focus again. I figured I knew what was going on. I had heard about this.

As I watched, one criminal apparently traveled into the future, because he came out of the booth with a silver foil suit, an overdeveloped forehead, and 8000 dollars in currency that was no good here. He had a futuristic ray gun, which he tried out on a pedestrian, instantly blasting him into fragments. Everyone laughed except the pedestrian. And I didn't laugh for long. It's actually not very funny, when you think about it. The next crook came out of the booth dragging a bucket full of Crown Jewels. Hey, I thought, these guys are doing all right.

I wanted to keep an eye on all this, but I didn't want to attract attention, so I pretended to be reading a newspaper. My act looked even more convincing when a newspaper blew up against my leg which I then used as a prop. It was evidently a newspaper brought back by one of the crooks from a different time period. It said it was from the year 2156 and the headline was "Apes Become Our Masters". The subhead was "Hollywood Right Again." And inside there was an editorial blasting the whole deal. Apparently, the apes took over after a series of increasingly violent peace demonstrations led to our unspeakably savage and bloody Universal Brotherhood and Love Thy Neighbor Wars.

I did a little of the crossword puzzle, (most of the answers were "Banana" or "Pretty Banana", so it was fairly easy) then looked up in time to see the last of the criminals coming out of the photo booth. Everyone else had had their turn and gone away with their spoils. This last one came out struggling under the weight of a small printing press that had "If Found Return To Johannes Gutenberg, 15th Century" painted on it.

The criminal was having trouble carrying both

the printing press and the briefcase, so he just tossed the briefcase off to one side. It landed on the hood of a parked car. This was exactly the sort of careless behavior that Groggins had been complaining about, and that I had been waiting for.

I watched the criminal lug his burden into the nearest pawnshop, which already had Watt's Steam Engine and George Washington's face in the window. Then I sprinted across the street, grabbed the briefcase off the hood of the car and made a beeline for my office.

CHAPTER ELEVEN

I sat down at my desk with a small, but measurable, and statistically significant, feeling of accomplishment. I hadn't solved the case I was working on, I had had my brains beaten out more times than I could remember, and I hadn't made any money in a month, but at least I got this damn thing. "I've got you anyway, PeeWee", I thought. You've got to take pleasure in whatever little triumphs you can in this life. Somebody on a bus told me that.

I was curious about what the time machine looked like, so I opened the briefcase. Inside was a very sophisticated looking machine that looked like a cross between a computer and something else, maybe another computer. I'm not sure what it was a cross between, but it sure looked like more than just one thing to me.

I fiddled with it a little bit, on the off chance that I might know what I was doing, but I didn't, and nothing happened. Then I started punching buttons at random, mostly just to have something to do. I was whistling and looking out the window as I punched them.

At some point I accidentally activated the machine and it started creating all kinds of time anomalies and time paradoxes. Those things that Groggins was worried about.

Somehow the time machine, as it vibrated across my desk, was moving backwards and forwards slightly in time and taking me with it. So, without meaning to, I was making copies of myself. There was the Me From A Minute Ago, the Me From A Minute From Now, the Me That Was Trying To Turn Off The Time Machine, the Me That Was Starting To Get Pissed, Me's all over the place. More Me's than were strictly necessary, or than you could ever use. I was also duplicating a gas bill that was on the desk near the machine.

After an hour or so, I had 3000 gas bills on my desk, and I was locking future and past versions of myself in the closet. "I'll let you all out when I get this sorted out," I told them. Another Me appeared, hand outstretched to shake, and I shoved him in the closet too.

I had to stop this or pretty soon I would need to rent a bigger office. I kept punching different buttons, turning the machine on an off, banging it on the table, and so on, but nothing worked.

I looked up at the clock on the wall. It was running in all sorts of directions, directions nobody ever heard of. Time was all screwed up. I made one last attempt to fix the machine. I got out my screwdriver and made a needlepoint adjustment to the biggest and reddest, and therefore most important looking, valve. Then I stepped back to see if that had solved the problem, bumping into three more Me's who were dancing by waving straw hats. I picked up the time machine, tossed it in the corner and walked out. I didn't give a damn anymore.

I went down to the bar on the ground floor to drink. I wasn't getting paid enough to sort all this out. It wasn't my job to make the universe work right. If it was my job, where was my uniform? See what I mean? It didn't figure. I ordered half a dozen bourbons. That's how to deal with things you don't understand. Drown them. There were five more of me at the bar. We didn't look at each other.

After awhile I calmed down and returned to my office. I called up the Civil Defense Shelter and asked to talk to Groggins. They asked how I got out. They thought I was still in there.

"Well I'm not," I told them.

"Your dinner's getting cold."

"I don't care. Let me talk to the professor."

They connected me and, with the criminals craftily listening in on the extension, I explained to Professor Groggins what I had inadvertently done. He was concerned about all the time paradoxes I had created. He warned me to be careful. I said it was a little late for careful. What we needed now was damage control, some story we could give to the press, and a fall guy.

While Groggins was cussing me out and telling me a lot of things about my character that I already knew, and if you really want to bore me that's the way to do it, I noticed about a dozen copies of me were next to the phone trying to listen in.

One of them said: "What is he saying? Is it about us?"

"Piss off," I told them. They looked stunned, then filed out of the office with identical hurt expressions on their faces. Hey, I can't be nice to everybody.

I told Groggins to relax. This could all be fixed easily enough.

"Just tell me how to use the machine. I'll go back in time a couple of minutes and sort this all out. I've got to at least get rid of some of these gas bills. So how do you operate this thing?"

A criminal's voice came over the phone. "First you..." Then he stopped talking immediately, as if he had been told to shut up by some friends.

"What was that?" asked Groggins.

"I don't know. Sounded like someone telling someone else to shutup."

We listened to see if we could hear anything more, but aside from some heavy breathing, and a couple more shutups, the line was quiet. Groggins gave me a quick tutorial in the use of the machine; which buttons to push, how to set the dials, which fingers to cross, and so on.

"Remember to get in a phone booth or some similar confined space so you won't take things from the present back in time with you. It could have unforeseen consequences.

"I'm only going back a couple of minutes."

"Yes, but..."

I hung up and started setting the dials the way he had said to set them. Unfortunately I had to hurry because the police were banging on my door demanding entrance and the surrender of the time machine. I didn't know how they found out that I had it. Maybe one of those criminals had blabbed it. I saw Dodge's foot come through the bottom of the door, then his forehead come through the middle of the door. I didn't have much time.

I quickly punched in some numbers, then pressed the button. My office suddenly looked all shimmery and out of focus. I rubbed my eyes, which made everything more out of focus, so I stopped doing that. I was going back in time all right. The ride was pretty bumpy at first, until I stopped shaking the briefcase. I have these nervous habits.

The machine had a speaker and a voice kept coming out of it yelling frantically "you are going back in time! back in time! back in time!" until I found the button to turn the speaker off.

After awhile I was pretty sure I was going a lot farther back than I'd intended, but I didn't know enough about the machine to chance stopping it mid-trip. I figured wherever I ended up, I would just come right back. No problem. Who could stop me? No one could, that's who could. I was the Master Of Space And Time. Ha-ha.

When the world around me stopped shimmering and sharpened into focus again I figured my trip was over. That feeling was confirmed when the time machine stopped vibrating and printed out an invoice. I took a look at the bill and then tore it up. I'm not going to pay that. I looked around. I was still in my office, but it looked a lot newer. Also it was full of typists banging away on manual typewriters. They stopped typing for a moment and stared at me, then resumed their work. I didn't remember having all those typists. You'd think I'd remember something like that. I looked at the door. It said "International Radium Watch Dial & Asbestos Corporation. America's Fastest Growing Company." Never heard of it. Sounded like I should buy some stock in it though.

My desk had been moved to a different spot in my office and my 3000 gas bills, which had traveled back in time with me, were now in a pile on the floor. I guessed that was what Groggins was talking about, those "unforeseen consequences". I didn't see what was so terrible about it. The gas bills were just as likely to get paid on the floor as they were on my desk. I left them there. Later I asked him if this is what he had meant by "unforeseen consequences" and he said "yes".

I walked out of the office and took the elevator down to the street. The same guy was running the elevator, but instead of being an old geezer he was four years old. That gave me an uncomfortable feeling.

When I walked out of the building, I saw that the street was filled with old-fashioned cars and equally old-fashioned people. A calendar boy came by.

"Calendars!" he called. "Get your current calendars!"

I flagged him down. "Hey calendar boy!"

I bought the least expensive calendar he had—the pictures were disturbing and made you vaguely ill, hence the bargain price—and looked at the year. It said it was 1941. I didn't believe it. I turned to the month of February. It was 1941 on that page too.

I started walking down the street, still half checking out the calendar pages and accidentally bumped into Joe Dimaggio and Whirlaway. They were both from 1941, I remembered. That looked like confirmation, but I still couldn't really believe it.

So I spent the next half hour walking around asking people what year it was, and they kept telling me, and I kept saying "get outta here! It is not!" but they kept insisting it was.

I walked up to some people who were filming a movie on the street and asked Sydney Greenstreet and Humphrey Bogart what year it was and they both confirmed the date I had been told before. When I was leaving, shaking my head with amazement, I heard the director say: "Wait, maybe we should leave it in. Maybe it's great." But then some other guy said: "Naw, it stinks". And they started re-shooting the scene.

I went back up to my office and got there just in time to see the briefcase shimmer and then fade away. I had forgotten to set the emergency brake as I was carefully warned to do by Professor Groggins about fifty times. If you don't set the emergency brake, he warned me fifty times, the machine will return to its default time period after awhile. I nodded fifty times while he was saying this, but when the time came to actually set the emergency brake, I forgot. So I guess I dropped the ball there.

I stood around for a moment, feeling the empty air where the time machine had been. I waited patiently for it to come back, but, to make a long story short, it didn't. That meant I was stuck here more than half a century from home, with no way to get back. I didn't like the sound of that.

CHAPTER TWELVE

I took a walk around town. It was like I was living in a history book. A stinking history book. I never did like history when I was in school, and this wasn't increasing my fondness for the subject. History is over, I've always felt, let's move on. I suppose some people would have found it charming to suddenly find themselves in an earlier, simpler time, where everyone was friendly and stupid, but I didn't. Try getting your mail in a situation like that. It can't be done. The one thing that made me feel better was knowing that I had screwed up cases a lot worse than this before.

As I walked, I calmly took stock of my situation. Number one: I didn't have the time machine anymore. So, number two: I was doomed. I calmly tried to think of a number three. There wasn't a number three. Then I remembered something that had gotten me out of a lot of tight spots before— hysteria. It might work in this situation. I would give it a try. So I ran down the street screaming and waving my arms, then curled up in a ball on the sidewalk and rolled all over the place, yelling and gibbering. All this accomplished nothing. Hysteria, I discovered, didn't work in a situation like this. Make a note of that.

When I calmed down enough to get my tongue out of my windpipe, it came to me that a person in my situation needed the help of a scientist. Since I didn't have access to Professor Groggins, I went to a nearby physics laboratory and asked to talk to the guy with the biggest brain. There was a whispered conference amongst the physicists, tape measures, skull saws, and forceps were brought out, then finally one of them came forward to talk to me with a slight smirk on his face.

I outlined my problem for him, as best as I knew how. We quickly got into a shouting match, with him saying time travel couldn't be done, and me saying then explain my presence here asshole. So he said make me. And I said I sure would in just about a minute. Then he punched me in the stomach. When I got my breath back, we agreed to disagree, and I left. So much for the scientific approach.

I knew at the time that it didn't make a lot of sense, but I was getting kind of desperate and I needed to talk to Professor Groggins, so I went to a telegraph office with the idea of sending a telegram to 2003. I figured the worst that could happen would be I'd be out a couple of bucks and the rest of the telegram sending public would give me the horselaugh. Which is what happened, so I was right in a way. Score one for me.

The people behind the counter didn't know

what I was talking about at first. And they still didn't know what I was talking about a couple of hours later. They said they didn't know where to send my telegram.

While I was trying to get them to give it a try anyway—what the heck, I pointed out—the line behind me got really long and angry. It has always amazed me how angry people can get at my stupidity. How do they think I feel? They only have to be around me a couple of hours at a time. I've got me all day.

In the end, they flatly refused to send my telegram. I told them I was going to complain to somebody and they said that's what they'd do, so we left it like that.

While I was fuming outside of the telegraph office, debating whether or not to go back in and try it again, maybe this time claiming I had a gun, or claiming that I had had a gun the last time, but didn't now, I suddenly remembered the long and tedious explanations I had received from Professor Groggins about how the time machine worked. This opened up a whole new line of thought. Maybe I could describe the time machine well enough so that a local artisan here in this time period could build one for me.

I walked to a nearby gas station and discussed the matter with a likely looking mechanic. I had made a crude drawing of the briefcase and its contents. I showed it to the mechanic and asked him if he could build it.

"It's shaped like a briefcase," I told him, "but that's only part of the story. It's also got all sorts of wheels and blinking lights and things inside. As illustrated here. Because it's a time machine as well as a briefcase. It's two things in one."

He looked my drawing over and frowned. "Well I can build the briefcase easy enough, but I can only guess about what to put inside it. Some of these shapes you've drawn don't exist in nature."

"Do the best you can," I told him. "That's all anyone can ask."

With me looking over his shoulder and kind of rooting him on and shouting words of encouragement, and reminding him to hurry up, he fashioned something that looked a lot like my time machine. It had the same kind of blinking lights, dials to indicate the passage of years and so on. I didn't know how tricky stuff like this was, but I figured if the space/time continuum wasn't paying much attention today, if it was looking out the window or chatting on the phone with the fourth dimension or something, this might work.

I took the time machine outside, found a phone booth and got inside. Normally at this point I would have set the dials for September 14th, 2003, but this version didn't have dials like that. There was just a space for me to write the date in with a grease pencil. I did so and turned on the machine.

The blast shot me out of the phone booth and halfway down the street, where I banged off a parked car.

When I regained consciousness, I asked the nearest gawker what year it was. He told me that it was 1941. March 14th · The same day it had been when I had left. I looked at my watch. It was 4:30 in the afternoon. That meant five hours had passed. I was pretty satisfied with that. Five hours closer to home, I thought. It's a start. Hot dog.

But my excitement faded when a street urchin who was sitting on the curb next to me blowing bubbles informed me that I had been laying on the asphalt bleeding for five hours. So the machine hadn't actually propelled me forward in time, it had just knocked me out for most of the day. A hammer could have done that. I went back to the gas station, full of righteous indignation and buyer's remorse.

I slapped the "time machine" down in front of the "mechanic" and informed him that it didn't work. I mean, not at all. He said he was sorry.

"Sorry doesn't get me back to 2003," I said, waggling a finger at the man. "This is a lemon. I'm not paying you for this. Do they have a Better Business Bureau in this time period?"

He hesitated for a moment, moved sideways to the left to block my view of something, then said no, there wasn't one. Lucky for him.

CHAPTER THIRTEEN

It was getting late in the day, and was starting to turn cold. I realized I had a more immediate problem than just getting home someday. I needed food and shelter, kind of nowish. I checked in my pockets to see how much cash I had with me. No problem there. I had $180 in bills, a pocket full of coins, and my credit cards and checkbook. And your money goes farther in the past, I've been told. So I figured I was set.

I approached the registration desk at the nearest five star hotel—unaccountably named the PreWar Hilton—and explained that I wished to get a room. They asked how long I would be staying and I said no more than 62 years, hopefully less.

While I was signing in the clerk was eyeing my clothes, which looked a little out of place in this era and had been kind of blown up recently. He said he would have to ask me for an advance deposit. This was no problem. When you have a causal attitude towards fashion, as I do, you get used to the better class of people, like clerks, treating you like garbage. Besides, I had nothing to worry about. I was loaded.

I handed the clerk a hundred dollar bill. He started to put it in the till, then looked closer at it. After a moment, he called some other people over to look at it. I was glad everyone in the hotel was finding out how well-heeled I was. You get better service that way. Next the assistant manager and then the manager were called over to examine the bill. The manager glanced at it, then studied it more closely, hissing slightly.

He looked at me. "Where did you get this 'money'?"

"I dunno. What does it matter as long as its money?"

"It's not money."

I scratched my head. "We're saying different things."

The manager said my bill wasn't redeemable in lawful money. It couldn't be exchanged for silver or gold, according to the words printed on the bill. It was just fiat currency. It wasn't good here, or anywhere.

"Bullshit," I said.

The manager shook his head. "It's not bullshit, I assure you, sir. Far from bullshit."

The assistant manager chimed in: "Mr. Jorgenson doesn't bullshit customers unless he absolutely has to. That's a credo he lives by."

A tough looking bellhop came up, angrily balling up his fists. "Who's questioning Mr. Jorgenson's integrity?" he asked.

The manager tried to defuse the situation, to

get us all to calm down. "That's all right, John. I can handle this."

Then they noticed the date on the bill. It had been printed in 1994. Now they really didn't like it. 1994 hadn't happened yet, they felt. I hopefully laid out the rest of my money on the counter, and invited them to take their pick. They didn't like any of those bills either. Then, after they had called the bank about the check I tried to write them and were told that my checking account didn't exist on this planet, and had stared at my American Express card for several minutes without comprehension, they began to lose all confidence in me as a customer.

They had a brief meeting, to which I was not invited, then gave me the bum's rush out into the street, hinting I should never return.

While I was picking myself up off the pavement and dusting myself off, a couple of policemen arrived and asked if I was Frank Burly, the guy trying to pass the funny money. I said I was, and asked their names. They grabbed one of my arms each and escorted me to their squad car.

They kept me in a cell for a couple hours, during which time I learned from another inmate how to kill a man with a walnut. No time spent with a man who knows his craft is wasted. Then they pulled me out for interrogation. I sat down in the interrogation room. Somebody had been eating their lunch in there and there was, among other things, a walnut on the table. I picked it up. You never know.

Fortunately, the police lieutenant who was

questioning me was a science fiction fan, so he was eager to believe my story. After I told him all about the world of the future, with it's death rays, rocket cars and flying nuns, he was putty in my hands. I knew the kinds of things he wanted to hear.

He asked if the Martians were ever going to attack the Earth. I nodded and said 1958. I said the Martians were tougher than the Crab Monsters and the Ghost Robots From The 2ND Dimension (Width), but that we managed to beat them in the end by tying their feelers together and screaming in their floppy ears until their brightly colored asses blew off. That satisfied him a lot. It gave him a real good feeling about Man's Fighting Future. I also told him that in the future all the women wore really short pants, shorter than was safe, a fashion development which I was prepared to sketch for him. He ate it up. This was great. All his suspicions were confirmed. Hooray for me and the future.

He agreed to let me go if I would write down all the World Series winners for the next 62 years for him. I tried to look reluctant and said I kind of owed it to the space/time continuum not to divulge important crap like that. His face fell and it looked like he was about to toss me back in the can again, so I communed with myself and said I guessed it would be all right. As long as he didn't share this important information about the future with other people at the casino. He agreed enthusiastically.

I wrote down all the winners for him, neglecting

to write down the fact that I don't remember that kind of stuff very well. I'm not even sure there is a baseball team named the Blue Pants. And I didn't tell him that I knew he was destined to get killed a year later in one of those police station cave-ins. I've always thought people shouldn't know too much about their future. Especially people who are about to let me go.

I handed over the list and was released immediately, with profuse apologies. They expressed the hope that I held no hard feelings towards them. They pointed out that they were only doing their jobs, and that this was a career their parents had chosen for them. They had wanted to grow up to be nice men, like me. I said that far from having hard feelings, I planned to name my first child after their police department: Coppertina if it was a girl, Fuzzy if it was a boy.

So we parted on amicable terms. The lieutenant shook my hand and got his picture taken with me, making out in the photograph like we were great buddies who went everywhere together. We vowed to visit each other often in the future, not just when I was being arrested. Then he hurried off towards a casino.

I sat down on a park bench to enjoy my freedom and mull over my financial situation. This, I could see, was going to be a problem. All my money was either paper that couldn't be redeemed in lawful money, or "silver" that wasn't made of silver. The only money in my pocket that was worth what it said it was, that had any intrinsic value, was a nickel and eight pennies. At least they were made of the metal they claimed to be. But 13 cents won't buy much, not even in 1941. And the coins I had were all minted in the 1980's and 90's anyway. I might be able to con a blind man out of something with them, but I could probably do that with a handful of gravel.

That 13 cents was probably going to have to last me a long time, unfortunately. No matter how I doped out the situation it looked like I was going to have to get back to 2003 the hard way, by living the whole 62 years. Which meant I'd be about 100 years old when I got back to my detective business. I might not be so burly by then. Might have to change my name. Frank Rickety, or Frank Coughy, or something. I'd still be frank with my clients though, so my first name wouldn't have to change.

Thinking about this gave me the answer. I could make money here the same way I had been making it in 2003. They had plenty of crime in 1941, if motion pictures were accurate sources of information. I'd just set myself up as a detective here, and wait for the space/time continuum to make a mistake and give me an opportunity to get back home.

I looked at my watch. It was too late to start being a detective today. The sun was going down and people were heading for home. They wouldn't need any detectives until tomorrow morning at 5 a.m. at the earliest. So what was I going to do for food and shelter tonight? I saw a drunk across the street weaving into a particularly rundown and inexpensive looking hotel called The Colossal-Majestic.

The roof of The Colossal-Majestic was sagging and a lot of the windows were out, and while I was looking at it an entire layer of paint peeled off and a bed slid out of a window and landed in the alley. A sign out front of the hotel said "Rooms With Heat: $2 A Night. Rooms Without Heat: $1. Rooms Without Anything: Ten Cents A Night." Another sign said "We Don't Examine Money Very Closely". This was the hotel for me.

CHAPTER FOURTEEN

I woke up the next morning cold and cramped. The room, as advertised, was a miracle of understatement. No heat, no lights, no blankets, no bed, just me. I washed my face in some snow that had drifted in through the window, and dried it on a handy rodent. Then, refreshed, disheveled, smelly, and hopeful, I headed out to make my mark in prewar America.

I found a likely looking street corner, one with lots of foot traffic and no competing detectives, and began accosting passersby, asking them if they had any crimes that needed solving today.

"Detective?" I yelled. "Crime solved, mister? Trace something for you, ma'am? Who else wants a detective?"

Business was bad at first. Everyone was evidently satisfied with their current detective. But I finally attracted the attention of a man who, as luck would have it, was actually on his way downtown to hire a detective. This chance meeting would save him some shoe leather, he informed me, rubbing his hands. He asked me if I came highly recommended and I said I sure as hell did. That was all he needed to know, and he started explaining his problem to me.

Unfortunately, the lunch hour was just starting and the foot traffic on my street corner suddenly increased. Pedestrians kept pushing their way between us, and a street vendor rolled up and set up shop next to us, yelling out the good news that he had peanuts for sale.

My prospective client asked me: "Do you have someplace else we could talk? Someplace quieter? Like an office?"

I told him yes, I did have an office, but we couldn't use it right now. He asked me why not and we stared at each other until both of us started to go to sleep. Finally he realized I was never going to answer him.

"Well, we'll do it here then," he said. "The thing I want you to investigate is connected with the Danielson Case."

"What's that?"

"You know, the ferry boat scandal over in Marina City."

"Where's that?"

"Never mind."

So I lost my first client. I realized I was going to have to bone up on the current events and geography around here if I was ever going to be of any value to my clients. I made a mental note to see if there was a library in this town.

While I was making, and admiring, this mental note, a cop nudged me with his nightstick.

"Move along," he said. "You can't be a detective here."

I didn't want any more trouble with the police, so I moved to an area where no pedestrians were walking, which satisfied the cop, but made it harder for me to conduct my business. I could yell and wave at passersby to come over to where I was in the flowerbed, but no one seemed to want to do that. If anything, they moved farther away from me the louder I shouted and the more I waved and made faces at them.

I reassessed my situation. It was clear that if I was going to be a successful detective here, I needed an office. That would cost money. And I'd need furnishings; a desk, file cabinets, a client chair, and so on.

That meant that at least for awhile, I was going to have to get some other kind of job, a less glamorous job, until I could build up some capital. This was a little depressing for me, because I like the power and prestige that goes with being a shamus more than the power and prestige that goes with, say, pushing a mop. But I cheered up when I remembered that I was the Man From The Future. I was 62 years ahead of these pre-1950 yokels mentally. I'd wow 'em back here in the primitive past.

The first thing I did was check out the want-ads in the paper. But I was in for a disappointment there. Every job seemed to require some experience or skills I lacked. Do you know how to be the comptroller for a canning company? Or how to build infernal machines for Anarchists? I don't.

And the lowest level jobs were out too, because they insisted that I not have some of the qualifications I did have. Like they didn't want me to have more than a third grade education, because they felt that if I had a fourth grade education, or its equivalent, I wouldn't be carrying sewer pipes for them very long. It would just be a pit stop for me professionally. So it seemed I was overqualified for some jobs, and underqualified for the rest. The general impression I got was that 1941 could get along perfectly well without me.

But if there's one thing you can say about us Burlys (okay, Torgesons. See chapter 1), it's that we don't give up right away. We don't give up for months. So I went out on a series of job interviews and tried to bluff my way through them, saying yes I was a fully qualified whatever-you-said, or no, I've never heard of the Union movement, what's that?—whatever I guessed they wanted to hear. Lying like this works pretty well, I've always found. Because it allows you to tell a prospective employer things you could never tell him if you were being truthful. But you tell that to the youth of today and they won't listen. They think they know it all.

The only times I ran into trouble were when I didn't lie. Like when I inadvertently filled out employment application forms with accurate information. My birth date, for example, raised a lot of red flags.

"Born in 1965, eh?" some personnel guy would say.

"Yes."

"I guess that makes you about minus 24 years old."

"I'm more mature than my age would indicate."

Sometimes I'd get over all the other hurdles and they'd take me out to the work site to see me in action before they hired me. To see me demonstrate the expertise I had bragged about on my application form. This was a problem, because it's easier to bluff your way through a written test than it is to bluff your way through real life.

They would ask me, for example, to run along a steel girder 20 stories above the pavement carrying a bucket of rivets. And I would, using this same example, fall off. So there goes that job.

But just when I was thinking I'd never be able to make any money in this time period, I found exactly what I was looking for. I was walking down the street, fingering the 3 cents I had in my pocket and discovering that I now only had 2 cents because I had fingered one of them to pieces, when I passed by a window with a sign in it that said "Day Jobs: No Experience Necessary". Other signs in the window were even more encouraging. "No Experience? No Problem!", "Prison Record? Hooray!", "Can't Read? Read This!"

I went inside and in almost no time I was earning real 1941 style money. My first job involved being set on fire in a vacant lot so the fire department could practice putting people out. I made five dollars doing that. And the sign in the window was right. No experience was necessary. All I had to do was stand there and scream. Anybody can do that.

CHAPTER FIFTEEN

Things were looking up for me now. I had five dollars. But I felt I was making money too slowly and painfully, and they hadn't discovered antibiotics yet. This was what gave me my big idea.

It occurred to me that the big advantage I had here in the past was that I knew what the future was going to look like. None of these jackasses did. I had been to the future, and even taken a picture of it. I could use that advance knowledge to make myself rich overnight. All I had to do was pick out something that was common in my time but wasn't available here yet, and then "invent" it. It would be hard luck on whoever was destined to really invent the thing, but I figured screw him.

I got some sheets of writing paper from the lobby in my hotel, then started writing down all the things I'd noticed weren't available in these primitive days. The list was surprisingly long, starting with the ball point pen I asked the guy behind the registry desk for. He'd never heard of such a thing and looked at me like I was a witch. So I settled for a pencil.

1941, I wrote, didn't have ball point pens, transistors, long playing records, TV dinners, electric toothbrushes, push button telephones, tubeless tires, microwaves, penicillin, VCRs, or almost anything made out of aluminum or plastic. Those were still exotic materials in this time period. Practically everything in 1941 was made of iron, wood, glass, or mud.

For the next few nights I worked feverishly, spending all my spare time and all the money I was making on my day jobs, trying to build a high definition television. Finally I gave up on that and switched to a ball point pen. After my prototype had flown to pieces for the fourteenth time, embedding the little ball in my cheek for the ninth time, I pushed all my inventing equipment out of the window and went out to get drunk. At least I had the skill to do that.

I hadn't realized that I never actually had a clue as to how any of the inventions of my era worked. Why hadn't somebody told me I was ignorant? What was the big secret?

After I'd had a few beers, and had taken out my anger and frustration on some smaller drunks, I started to cheer up again. I realized the mistake I had made was in trying to duplicate the actual important achievements of my time, the things that made life better, the things with moving parts. I could make just as much money, maybe more, by duplicating the crap of my era.

So I got to work again, trying to cash in, in

advance, on some of the nationwide fads that I knew were coming. Davy Crockett hats, disco, that sort of thing. But I'll tell you a secret—most people wouldn't tell you this, but I will. I'm your friend— it's hard to get a nationwide fad going. The nation is a big place. You can get, say, Cincinnati whipped into a frenzy about your product, but just as you're just finishing that, now Detroit is starting to calm down, so you have to run back there. The whole thing is harder than it sounds.

After two weeks of work, all I had managed to sell were three Davy Crockett Caps, two Ralph Kramden Bus Driver Games, and one recording of me singing "Stayin' Alive". And the people who bought them weren't very excited about their purchases after awhile, and a couple of them wanted to sell them back to me, but I wasn't interested.

I'd like to report to you that it wasn't long after this that I figured a way out of my predicament and got back to the good old present day, but it didn't turn out to be that easy. It was eight long months before my chance came to get home.

I spent those eight months continuing to earn a small humiliating living doing day jobs. I never could quite get enough money saved up to get my detective business going, mostly because I kept coming up with brilliant ways to triple my money overnight. I kept thinking I could remember which Bum Of The Month was going to beat Joe Louis, but it was never any of the guys I put money on. So I had to keep starting over. I pushed mops all over 1941, passed out handbills, posed for "Before" pictures, and so on. My one big payday was a one-day gig I had doing a cameo appearance in the movie The Pride Of The Yankees. In the scene where Lou Gehrig finds out he's dying, I'm the guy who's pointing at him and laughing.

To save money I tried living with my grandparents for awhile, but they were uncomfortable having me around. I kept hearing them muttering things like "It's not natural", "Who is he?" and "Space/time continuum". So after a couple of weeks I split.

One money making idea I had during this period promised to be a gold mine for me. I wrote out motion picture scripts that were word for word transcriptions of successful films I had seen in the 1990's, then shipped them off to Hollywood and sat back to wait for the checks to come rolling in. All the scripts were returned to me, with rejection slips that said they stunk to high heaven. I read the scripts again and they did! This made me mad on several levels.

Despite my shortage of money, life in 1941 wasn't too bad. Like I said before, I'm not a history buff, but the past did have its charms. The food didn't have any preservatives or vitamins in it, so it had a pleasant, dangerous taste that was new to me. There weren't any safety rules anywhere, so if you hurt yourself, at least you didn't get yelled at too. And the whole year was in full natural color, not the grainy black and white I was led to expect. It was all kind of pleasant. A restful period in our history to be alive, I felt. It's true that there was a war going on in Europe, but Europe was a long ways away. You couldn't hear any of the screaming where I was.

The only time the war entered my life at all in those days was the afternoon I was walking down the street and Rudolf Hess landed on me. I told him he was supposed to land in Scotland, not on top of me, and I expected the Third Reich to replace my hat with one just as good. I hinted that otherwise there would be trouble. Germany was already fighting with France and England. They didn't want to piss me off too.

He tried to surrender to me, but I didn't have any facilities for housing any prisoners at that time. He would have had to sleep in my bed with me. So I told him he'd better just move along. He wandered off, dragging his parachute behind him, looking back at me like I was a jerk or something. The feeling is mutual, pal. I guess he eventually got to Scotland and lost the war for his country all right.

I wasn't the only person who was ignoring the war. Nobody in our town was interested. It was too far away, and no one liked those Europes anyway. The thing the people in our town wanted to talk about—the thing that really got the newspapers excited—was the race for District Attorney. This race looked like it was going to be not so much an election, but a coronation, for the incumbent, a guy by the name of Mandible, oddly enough. I wondered if he was any relation. He was the most popular man in the city, and everyone from the Mayor down was stumping for him. But I wasn't really following the election. I wasn't eligible to vote in this time period anyway, not being alive in any way that could be measured.

Most of my leisure time was spent in bars, where I would regale the locals with my exciting tales of the future.

"In the future," I informed my slack-jawed audience, "there will be gas pumps that talk."

"What will they talk about?" hushed voices would ask.

"Gas."

This didn't seem so much unbelievable as boring to them.

"So?" asked one of them.

"So, that's something that I know and you don't know. Advantage, me."

This got them confused. "But you just told us all about it," said one.

"Everybody in the place knows it now," said another.

"We can't stop thinking about it at this point," added a third.

My superior grin faded into an equal scowl. They were right. I vowed not to tell them any more about the future. Why should I give away my advantage? But it's hard not to show off how smart you are. All smart guys know this. After a couple more drinks I was back to dispensing knowledge again.

"In the future," I intoned, "there will be fins on cars. Then they will be gone. And someday there will be a man named Hitler or Hister who will cause a great war..."

Someone raised their hand. "You mean that war that's been going on in Europe for the last two years?"

"Yes!" I said impressively.

The more I talked about the future, the more interested they got. "What's going to happen in 1977?" asked one.

"I forget."

"How about 1978?"

"Forget. Wait, I think I remember something... no, it's gone."

"Gee, the future sounds real exciting," one of the drunks sneered.

"Hey, lay off the future," I warned him. "It's all right."

Sometimes I got competition from other drunks in the bar who claimed they were from a more interesting future than I was.

"In the future I'm from," said one drunk in the back, "everybody is movie stars. And we're all married to Carole Lombard. And our dogs crap money."

I didn't remember any of that, and doubted that this man had ever traveled to the future at all, but he certainly had a more riveting story to tell than I did. After awhile I found myself making up stuff too. I didn't feel good about that, but I didn't want to lose my audience. Once you've been the center of attention, it's hard to go back to being one of the guys in the corner.

Through all of this, I never gave up trying to find a way to get back to 2003. I made it a point to always stand within five feet of anyone I saw carrying a briefcase, just on the off chance he was a time traveler. I haunted briefcase stores. I even listened to The Briefcase Hour on the radio for awhile. But that was a stretch, and the show was pretty terrible so I switched to Edgar Bergen.

Once, in desperation, I tried to attract attention to my plight by damaging the space/time continuum, figuring science would eventually trace the problem back to me. So I booed the hell out of Citizen Kane Part Two, the film that focuses on what Kane said after "Rosebud"—all those long sentences he yelled out real fast at the end there, and that song he sang—trying to make the movie into a flop, instead of the biggest blockbuster in film sequel history. I figured future film critics would sense something was wrong, alert the scientific community, and maybe come to my rescue somehow. It flopped all right, thanks to me, but no film critics ever showed up. Lazy bastards.

But I did finally find a way back home. All I had to do was look across the street at the right moment.

I was in the middle of one of my humiliating day jobs, pigeon cleaning duty for the city—I especially hated brushing their filthy little teeth and combing their ratty fur. And where were their wings? That's what I wanted to know—when I looked up at the right moment to see an elevator suddenly appear on the sidewalk and Big Al Pellagra get out and start walking purposefully across the street. Under his arm was a figurine of Justice Holding The Scales.

CHAPTER SIXTEEN

I dropped the pigeon I had been spit-shining, rushed over to the elevator, and stepped inside. The briefcase was there! Excitedly, I started fiddling with the dials, then I stopped. I couldn't just hurtle off through time and leave the figurine here. I was being paid to recover it. In theory, anyway. Also, I was a little curious. Why would Pellagra have traveled 62 years into the past to where I was, carrying the figurine I was looking for, and walk right past me with it? Coincidences of that magnitude make me stiffen slightly. And what was Pellagra planning to do with the figurine now that he was here? I had to find out.

I stepped out of the elevator, put the briefcase in a stray dog's mouth and told him to "stay", then thought better of it and put the briefcase back in the elevator. Then I started to follow Pellagra.

I kept behind him, but at a discrete distance until he walked up the steps into the police station. I decided to wait outside. There were policemen in there. After a few minutes he came

101

back out, no longer carrying the figurine. He looked around at all the old cars and the unfamiliar skyline with a slightly bemused expression, then saw a diner advertising a strictly 1940's Italian dish called LaSpaghettiloni. He licked his lips, looked at his watch, smiled as if realizing it didn't really matter to a time traveler what time it was at any particular moment, then went into the diner and sat down. I headed into the police station.

I walked up to the desk sergeant and pointed at the figurine which was perched on the desk next to him.

"Can I have that?" I asked.

He said I couldn't have it. It was important evidence. "Who are you anyway, and what do you want?"

I said I was a friend. A friend who wanted that thing that was on his desk. I offered to buy it. His whole attitude changed.

He said I couldn't have the figurine, but just about everything else in the police station was for sale. He started showing me stuff that I could buy and quoting me special prices that he felt were a real steal for evidence of this quality, but I insisted I only wanted the figurine. We were at an impasse.

I asked to see my lieutenant friend, the one who liked the future even more than I did. He would go to bat for me and help put this deal across. The desk sergeant said the lieutenant was on extended leave. He had embezzled the police pension fund and bet it all on the Red Faces to win the 1941 World Series, as per the list I had given him. The Red Faces, hampered by the fact that they didn't exist, did not win, and the lieutenant's star had faded here at the station.

While the desk sergeant was telling me all this, I slowly tried to steal the figurine. My hand inched ever closer to it, but just before I got hold of it, the desk sergeant picked it up and handed it to another policeman. "Put this in the evidence room," he said.

The policeman took it and walked off. After he had gone I looked at the desk sergeant.

"Where's the evidence room?" I asked. "Is it near here?"

He didn't say anything. I pointed. "I know it's down that corridor. Then should I turn left or right?"

"Hey, who are you?" he asked.

"You want my real name or my other name?"

"Take your pick."

"Burly."

Two big cops hustled me out of the building and threw me down the steps. "Get out Burly," one of them said.

I picked myself up and started heading back towards the elevator. I figured I'd given it my best shot. Now to get back to 2003 where I belonged. At least I could tell Mandible where the figurine was, so I had accomplished part of my mission.

I got into the elevator and activated the time machine. The elevator started to shimmer but just as it was beginning to disappear into time, Big Al Pellagra stepped in.

We looked at each other, startled. But before

we could react to each other's surprise presence, the elevator began heading for home. Pellagra and I looked straight ahead during the journey like two strangers on an elevator should. Our eyes strayed towards each other occasionally, but then darted away.

The elevator arrived in 2003 and the door opened. Both of us got out without saying anything and we went off in opposite directions. I had the presence of mind to keep hold of the briefcase.

CHAPTER SEVENTEEN

I arrived at my office building and immediately ducked behind a parked police car. There were dozens of police cars parked all around my building. Some of them with their sirens howling. Sgt. Dodge, who was in charge of the operation, was walking around trying to find out whose police cars those were and get them to shut their sirens off.

"This is a covert operation, people!" he shouted over his bullhorn. "Covert!"

About 35 cops were crowded into the front entryway to my building, looking sharply around for any signs of me. Hundreds more were on the roof. And a couple of cops were climbing up and down the face of the building—walking a very tough beat if you ask me.

It had been so long, I had forgotten the cops were trying to get that time machine away from me. It hadn't been a long time for them. Only half an hour had gone by for Sgt. Dodge since he had battered down the door to my office and watched me disappearing into the past, so that disappointment was still fresh in his memory.

One of the cops saw me crouching behind his car and yelled at me to get out of there. This was a restricted area, he informed me. Police personnel only. I was about to tell him that I had a perfect right to be here because I was the guy the cops were looking for. I was a real major player in this drama. But I decided it would be wiser to remain silent. I'd let him win this round.

I backed away from the building without being seen and yelled at more than two or three more times, then stashed the time machine at my house, and went off to see Mandible.

I gave a complete verbal report of what I'd done over the past eight months to Mandible and his new junkie secretary, who was taking frantic and self-destructive notes of the meeting. Mandible was fascinated by my story whenever the figurine or Pellagra was mentioned, but didn't seem interested in the rest of it—my months of hardship, the binge drinking, the moments of self-doubt, and so on. I thought those were the most interesting parts of the story, and sort of acted out some of them, doing all the voices, but Mandible just made "hurry up" motions with his hand during those parts of the story, which he characterized as "drivel", and told me to "skip on down" to the important stuff.

When I had finished my report, Mandible seemed satisfied. He wasn't upset at all that I hadn't gotten the figurine, he said, because I was going to go back there right now and get it.

"Bring it back here, or destroy it," he said. "Either way. It doesn't really matter."

This confused me. "Hey, do you want this thing or not?"

"I want it. But if I can't have it, I don't want anyone to have it."

I could understand that. I feel that way about everything. But I didn't fancy the idea of going back to 1941. It had been a bad year for me. So I said no, I'd remain here, if it was all the same to the universe, if space and time didn't mind.

Mandible insisted. He said if I didn't do what he wanted he would horsewhip me. I asked where he was going to get a horsewhip at this time of day? All the horsewhip stores were closed. He must have realized the truth of this because he changed his tack. He started pleading with me to go back, pointing out that he was an old man, a pathetic figure with a whiny insistent voice. I should have mercy on him and do what he wanted or he'd by God horsewhip me.

I told him I wouldn't even consider going back unless somebody told me what this whole thing was all about. When you've been played for a sucker as many times as I have, you start to get a sense of when it's happening again. It's like radar or something. There was something missing from this story, my sucker-sense told me. Mandible seemed like about the least sentimental guy I'd ever met, and I've met some people who have been dead for a week. So why did he really want this figurine so much, if it wasn't sentiment? I wanted the whole story this time. And even if I got it, I cautioned, I wasn't promising anything. I wasn't either.

He blustered for a little while longer, referring back to the horsewhip once or twice, then finally relented.

"No one outside the family has ever known the full story," he said. "You must swear you'll never reveal a word of what I'm about to tell you to anyone."

I said sure, you got it, Ace. And I meant it, too. But the thing people should know about me when they swear me to secrecy is that I don't have a good memory. The first thing I forget is that it's a secret. The second thing I forget is who told me this secret. The third and final thing I forget is the secret itself. So if you tell me something in the strictest secrecy, you're guaranteeing that eventually everyone in the world will know this secret except me.

I probably should have mentioned this to Mandible, but I really wanted to know what was going on, however briefly. So I said he could rely on my discretion. He took a deep, reluctant breath, then began telling me the story.

His grandfather, he told me, was Thomas Dewey Mandible the 1st. Tom Mandible had only done one bad thing in his life. But that one bad thing had made him a fortune.

He had been a low-level building inspector for the city, when he was approached by the Pellagra Crime Family and offered a series of gigantic bribes to look the other way and whistle when building permits were issued to a group of disreputable firms that were secretly owned by the Pellagras. These firms were known for their faulty construction techniques, shoddy building materials, and spectacular profit margins.

Their buildings were dangerous, stupid, and surprisingly inexpensive to construct for something so stupid. Among their most infamous creations were the futuristic looking, but doomed to collapse, Skyscraper Of Cards, which was made entirely of giant slabs of playing card material which were just kind of leaning against each other hopefully, and the Balloon Building, which was made of 100% balloon alloy. Their claim that balloon material was 50% stronger than tempered steel, which explained why they had to charge the city 80% more, was 0% true. In the three months following its dedication, the building kept slowly getting smaller and losing its shape, until finally somebody stepped on it.

The Pellagras were at the forefront of what has been called the Golden Age Of Criminal Architecture. Their buildings didn't stay up for long; some only lasted a couple of days before the wind knocked them over, or some wise guy kicked the first story out from under the building. But that didn't bother the Pellagras. They'd already gotten their money. And it certainly didn't bother Thomas Dewey Mandible The 1st. He just took the money, stamped the permits, then chuckled all the way to the bank. But not to a bank constructed by the Pellagra family.

He became very rich very fast. After this, he never did another dishonest thing in his life, partly because he didn't have to, but mostly because of vanity. Now that he was rich, he wanted to be respected, even beloved, by all.

So he built libraries, gave the city art museums, erected statues of honest and semi-honest Americans, turned worthless slum areas into money-making parks, and of course, made sure to put his name on everything; Mandible Park, Mandible Library, Mandible Police Station and so on.

And it worked. The people loved him. He led every 4th of July and Founders Day parade, usually riding in a big red fire engine. And when the people cheered, they weren't cheering American Independence or our city's founding fathers, they were cheering him.

The only flaw in this idyllic picture was that the town that loved Tom Mandible was an imperfect town. Crime was rampant. It wasn't safe to walk through Mandible Park at night, and you couldn't visit certain sections of Mandible Library without getting shot.

So, he decided to single-handedly clean up the city. He used some of his ill gotten gains to finance his election to the position of District Attorney. With the millions he had to spend, his election was a walkover. His honest opponent bribed as many people as he could, but he never really had a chance. Mandible's pockets were too deep.

He then used his powerful position to vigorously prosecute criminals of all kinds, sending them away for long stretches in prison. He especially enjoyed prosecuting members of the

Pellagra crime family. He couldn't get them for bribery in his case, because that was a secret, shh!, but he could get them for everything else they did. And they were into everything. In one memorable month—February 1941—they had committed every crime in the United States.

1941 was an election year in our city, and with Tom Mandible up for reelection to the D.A. post, both the criminals and the opposition politicians were howling that he was almost as crooked as they were, and shouldn't be re-elected. Tom wasn't worried. He was the most revered man in the city. No one would believe these slanderous accusations against him. And he knew his opponents had no proof of his previous indiscretions. There was proof though.

He had always been a meticulous man. He kept exact records of everything, including the bribes he had taken. He had even had forms printed up to make the record keeping easier and more precise. The forms had blanks for "Amount Of Bribe Offered" "Bribee" "Briber" "Bribe Accepted By", "Magnitude Of Crime" etc. All carefully filled out. His opponents knew that someone as meticulous as he was would retain those records, even though they could be a danger to him. They decided to get their hands on them and expose him.

On the weekend before the election, the four sneakiest and stupidest members of the Pellagra family broke into Mandible's office and hunted for the evidence, looking in the filing cabinets under "C" for "Crooked Politician", "R" for "Our

112

Agreements", and "L" for "What We're Looking For".
They didn't find what they were looking for.

When Tom Mandible came in to his office on
Monday morning and saw the whole place
trashed, and all the file cabinets rifled, he
immediately realized what had happened and
what the criminals had been looking for. He took
the evidence out of the "B" drawer, toyed with the
idea of burning the papers, but couldn't bring
himself to do it. They were all filled out so nice
and neat, with no empty blanks or anything. So
he decided to keep them, but to disguise what
they were.

He took the papers to an origami shop and
had them fashioned into a figurine of Justice
Holding The Scales. They were then covered with
a light coat of gold enamel. You could still see the
words on the folded papers, but no incriminating
words were visible unless you took the figurine
apart. There was a sign forbidding that next to
the figurine.

He put the completed figurine on his desk and
kept it there for the rest of his life, sometimes
toying with it or having it fight other figurines,
but mostly just letting it sit there out in the open,
incriminating as hell. It amused him. Every time
someone was in his office, toying with or looking
at the figurine, not realizing its significance, he
would laugh to himself. He became known as The
Laughing To Himself D.A.

The family should have destroyed the figurine
after Tom died, but they liked his little joke as
much as he did, and didn't see how it could hurt

anything now. Not unless somebody invented a time machine and took the evidence back to 1941 and gave it to the cops, which they regarded as, at best, an 8 to 1 shot. So they kept it on the mantel in the family mansion and laughed so uproariously when people looked at it that people stopped looking at it.

But then a time machine was invented and crooks did get hold of it. This happened during what started as a routine burglary at Mandible Manor. One of the burglars, the current head of the Pellagra family, Big Al Pellagra, found the figurine on the mantel. He noticed his grandfather's name, still visible under the gold enamel, realized the figurine's significance, and then used the time machine to take the figurine back to 1941 and destroy Tom Mandible.

"And it did destroy him," said Mandible the 3rd, handing me an old yellowed newspaper clipping. I glanced over the story.

It told how Tom Mandible had lost his re-election bid by a wide margin, and was jailed for his now-revealed crimes. And the scandal did more than just ruin Mandible. It threw the entire anti-crime movement in the city into disrepute. Everyone in 1941 figured, well law and order doesn't work, let's let crime give it a try.

"That's why you must go back to 1941 and get that figurine before it's handed over to the police," Mandible said. "Otherwise you'll doom me to a life in the gutter, and I don't think you want that, and this city to a half century of rampant crime."

He waved a hand at the city, inviting me to look and see how the city had changed now that his grandfather was not there to bust up the crime syndicate.

I said: "I don't see anything different. Are we looking at the same thing?"

Mandible sneered at me for being an unobservant oaf, which, as I said before, I plead guilty to. There's not much that happens around this town that I notice. He said he would take me on a tour of the town himself and show me what he meant.

CHAPTER EIGHTEEN

As Mandible took me around the town, showing me what had happened to it now that his grandfather had never been in a position to nip the criminal syndicate in the bud, an amusing thought occurred to me. I have this humorous side to my nature. I guess this is as good a time as any to mention that. I had noticed that Mandible was sort of like the Ghost of Criminal Future! Showing me around, and so forth. I asked him if he'd read Dickens. He told me to shut my mouth. We didn't talk about literature any more after that. But I still think it was an amusing reference.

He was right about the city. It certainly had changed. I guess I should have noticed. What are people paying me for, anyway? Gone were all the things the Mandible family had built: the sports stadiums, the libraries, the civic auditoriums, the roller skating rinks, in fact every fun or interesting thing people did in this town. All of it had been replaced by whorehouses, gambling hells, opium dens, and all manner of other unsavory things.

The only thing left for a decent person to do on Saturday night was to get robbed. And robbed they were. Sometimes as often as twenty times an hour. Criminals were completely out in the open now. Policeman not only weren't arresting them, they were actually joining them.

"This is now a city where the police are as bad as the criminals," said Mandible "And where honest private investigators like you are harassed by corrupt policemen."

That was certainly something I had noticed. I frowned. He had a good point there. We've got to do something about that last thing, I thought.

I suggested Mandible go back in time and do all the dirty work himself. That would be better. I didn't like 1941, and it didn't like me. So he could go. I would stay here, sort of standing guard. He asked what he was paying me for? I reminded him that he hadn't actually paid me anything yet. He dismissed this as mere wordplay. He said he was too old to go gallivanting around time and space. I was young and strong and resourceful. Besides, there might be dangers. He needed to send someone who was expendable. I had to admit I was pretty expendable all right, now that I thought about it. Damned expendable.

He finally clinched the deal by upping the amount of money he was theoretically going to pay me, to double my normal rate. That sounded like money I could theoretically use, so I agreed.

But this time I was going to go back prepared. I went home and loaded up with all the things I'd wished I'd had the first time around. I started with a lot of cash, making sure that all the bills were printed before 1941. I got a nice warm coat, an almanac so I could win bar bets, and I also wrote down a good answer to give some guy I had been having an argument with back there. Then I took a shower, because I remembered that someone in 1941 had suggested I do so. Once I was absolutely sure I had packed everything, that nothing had been overlooked, I reached for the briefcase. It was gone. Someone had broken into my home and stolen it.

I probably should have noticed the muddy footprints on my floor before. They were all over the house. You practically couldn't see anything else. They led through the broken window, up to where I had stashed the briefcase, then into the kitchen. Following the muddy tracks, I saw that the intruder had made some lunch for himself, then doubled back to the living room where he apparently watched some of my videotapes, then into my bedroom for some jumping on the bed, then back to the living room where he left by a different broken window.

I would have been concerned, but since I knew what the burglar had stolen, I figured it wouldn't be too difficult for me to find it again.

I took a walk down the street, looking for something inexplicable. Sure enough, a couple of blocks from my house I saw an elevator suddenly appear on the sidewalk and a crook come out pulling a horse that had a medieval knight on it. About thirty crooks, and a few crooked cops were standing in line, waiting their turn with the machine.

I didn't hesitate. 'Always take time travelers by surprise', they say. While the crook was wrestling with the horse and dodging the lance blows of the knight, and telling the knight to either quit calling him a varlet or tell him what it meant, I hurried up to the elevator and, ignoring the line entirely, dove in and closed the door.

There was general outrage about this line-cutting. The crooks began pounding on the door. The cops in the line began blowing their whistles.

As quickly as I could, I set the dials for October 12, 1941, turned on the machine, and began hurtling back through time.

On an impulse I mooned most of the 1950's as I went by. I don't know what makes me do these things. I guess it's just part of my charm.

CHAPTER NINETEEN

The elevator shimmered to a stop. I got out and checked my watch. I had arrived, as planned, fifteen minutes before Pellagra was due to show up with the figurine. I didn't want him to see me when he did arrive, so I ducked behind a convenient pile of lumber.

After awhile I noticed there were two other detectives back there with me. They were watching some suspects across the street. One of the detectives made a motion to me. I returned the motion and that's when the scrap started. Nobody motions to me like that. In the ensuing struggle we knocked over some of the lumber and everyone in the street kind of knew we were there now. The suspects took off, and the two detectives ran after them, cussing. My fault, I guess.

I turned my attention back to the elevator just in time to see it disappear. I had failed to set the emergency brake again, but this time on purpose. The machine had to be available for Pellagra to use. I looked at my watch. Just a couple more minutes.

At this point I had a crisis of conscience. My conscience was telling me if I went through with this, I would be preventing a corrupt city official from paying the just penalty for his crimes. And that, my conscience stressed, practically waggling its finger, was wrong.

If you've read this much of my story you're probably wondering where the hell this conscience of mine came from all of a sudden? Where has it been all this time? I was wondering the same thing. Just what a detective needs in the middle of a difficult case is a complex ethical problem. I thought about it for a minute, then told my conscience to take the rest of the day off, go watch a movie or something. If it bothered me again, I'd beat its brains in. That's the way you have to deal with things like that. A firm hand. Otherwise you'll be taking orders from everybody.

Suddenly the elevator returned. Pellagra stepped out and started across the street, carrying the figurine exactly as he had before.

I took off after him. I wasn't planning to do anything tricky. I was just going to knock him down, grab the figurine, get back to the elevator and warp out of there before he knew what hit him. It probably would have worked like a charm too, except halfway across the street I ran into myself from the last time I was there and started fighting with myself, punching myself in the belly and getting punched in the belly in return. The fight, predictably, ended in a draw, and I ran off in different directions.

Later I asked Professor Groggins about this

fight. He said it couldn't have happened and showed me a bunch of equations to prove it. I ran the numbers a couple of times on my pocket calculator and they checked out. So I guess it didn't happen. But sometimes, when Groggins isn't around, when I'm alone in my room with the lights out, and my calculator's in the other room, I wonder if it did.

Because of this fight I thought I had, I was delayed in stopping Pellagra. So once again he had gotten into the police station with the figurine. The idea of going back to 2003 so I could come back and try the whole thing again just made my head hurt. The logistics of these things is what gets to you after awhile. I decided to just stay in 1941 and try to get the figurine away from the cops, using some tricky method I hadn't tried last time. That meant all I needed now was a trick to pull. Some kind of great trick. I thought for a minute, then pulled out my gun and marched into the police station.

Pointing a gun at the cops turned out to be a pretty good trick. Simple, yet effective. It saved everybody a lot of time and cut down on the backtalk. I had everybody in the police station reaching for the sky in no time. Pellagra too. He didn't seem very happy to see me there, but then no one ever seems to be, so my feelings weren't hurt. I picked up the figurine off the sergeant's desk and started to back out of the station, also grabbing a couple of other things that looked interesting.

"You'll never get away with this," said the desk sergeant.

"Yes I will. I've got the perfect alibi. I haven't been born yet."

The cops looked at each other. They were impressed. That was some alibi all right.

I ran out of the police station with the figurine. No one was pursuing me because I had told them that if any of them moved, or even lowered their hands, the bomb would explode. It was quite awhile before they realized, hey what bomb?

Just as I was nearing the elevator, I saw a cop standing there writing a ticket and looking for the machine's license plate. I ducked behind a parked car. Maybe he'd be gone in a minute, I thought. It doesn't take very long to write a ticket. Before that minute could pass, however, a strange looking machine shimmered into existence next to the elevator. It looked like it had started out life as a particularly large and menacing phone booth. But now it had a flashing red light on top of it and many guns sticking out of its gunports. It said "Time Machine - Mark VI" on it.

I found out later that Sgt. Dodge had gotten tired of only being able to pursue me when I happened to be in the year 2003. He had grabbed Professor Groggins and forced him to quickly slap together another time machine. One that was even bigger and faster than the one I was using. But then he loaded it down with all kinds of heavy armament, so in the end it was a little slower than the Mark V.

The door opened and Dodge and his boys emerged.

"Burly!" called Dodge. "Oh Burly boy! It's your old friend, Dodgy!"

I was trying to decide whether I should answer or not, when a cat halfway up the street coughed and Dodge and his boys whirled and lambasted it with automatic weapons fire, keeping it spinning in the air for over three minutes. I decided maybe it would be better for me to remain quiet for awhile. We were all a little too jumpy right now. And our aim was too good.

Dodge and his boys fanned out and started looking for me. I couldn't run anywhere without being seen immediately, and Dodge's men were getting close to my hiding place, so it looked like it wouldn't be long before they picked me up by the ears and said something like "Well well well, look what we've got here," which is a phrase I've learned to hate.

But before they could get to me, the police station across the street emptied out and a large contingent of 1941 cops ran up. The two groups of cops stared at each other. Dodge tapped his badge in a meaningful way.

"21st Century police," Dodge said. "We're looking for a fat guy named Burly."

"So are we," said the desk sergeant. "He just held up the police station."

"He's from our time period," said Dodge. "So we'll take it from here, if it's all right with you."

The desk sergeant frowned. "You can't do that. We've got jurisdiction here. This is our time period."

Dodge said: "Jurisdiction is a nice thing to have. But we're better equipped to handle this. We're the Cops Of The Future. We've got more sophisticated weapons and more advanced crime detection techniques at our disposal than you have."

"Yes," retorted the desk sergeant, "but you're weaker physically and you look stupid with those overdeveloped heads. No crook will take you seriously here. And let go of my face."

I watched, fascinated, as the two police forces argued about who was best equipped to bring me to justice. This was starting to get interesting. So instead of trying to escape like I should have, I poked my face over the fender of the car to get a better look at what was going on, and started eating a candy bar.

As I watched, the two groups of cops quickly went from showing each other their equipment, to test firing each weapon, to beating each other over the heads with their weapons. Pretty soon they were just tearing each other to pieces, rolling around and fighting, yelling "ya bastard! ya bastard!".

This was my chance. I bolted from my hiding place and headed for the elevator. I didn't say 'So long, suckers!' or 'See you in the funny papers', but I was thinking those things.

As soon as I broke cover, all fighting stopped and the two groups of cops lit out after me. I got to the elevator first, ran in and shut the door. Then I opened it again and stuck my head out to see how far away the cops were, and several of them ran into the elevator with me.

Somehow, in the ensuing struggle, the time machine started up and off we went into the void.

The rest of the cops jumped into the Mark VI and disappeared into time to give chase.

As we hurtled through the eons, the cops in my elevator were bashing me with billy clubs and stunning me with tasers, while the elevator was being fired on by the time machine that was following us. The figurine was on the floor of the elevator, forgotten by everyone, being kicked from one side of the elevator to the other and occasionally stepped on.

I won't bore you with a full account of my adventures through time and space because I know you are primarily interested in the crime solving aspects of this case. You are a student of criminology. And I respect you for that. But during the roughly nine months the chase went on, a number of interesting things happened that I probably should mention here.

The first time the time machine stopped and I was able to get out and make a run for it was in the year 1865.

The cops caught up to me at Ford's Theater. When they drew their guns and started to shoot, I ducked behind Abe Lincoln. Now, I know what you're going to say: faux pas. I won't deny it. But I mean, what the heck, he was going to die anyway, right? As it turned out, he wasn't much of a shield. The automatic weapons fire practically tore both him and John Wilkes Booth in half.

While the cops were arguing with Secret Service Men and historians, I ran back to the time machine. Some of my pursuers dove in just as I was pulling away and resumed wrestling with me for control of the machine.

We next arrived in Hollywood in 1919, and they chased me all over that town. There were a lot of filmmakers roaming the streets in those days looking for something cheap and interesting to film so, without knowing we were doing it, we inadvertently made some pretty good Keystone Kops pictures. I've got a stack of royalty checks on my desk right now for work I didn't really do. I mean, I wasn't really trying to entertain anybody. I was just trying, in my own way, to escape.

At one point I managed to get the elevator to myself and, trying to throw the cops off the scent, I traveled far into Earth's future, where all was peace and harmony and everyone was perfect and snotty. I didn't fit in too well there. They viewed me as some kind of Neanderthal, because my forehead didn't weigh 80 pounds like theirs did, so they chucked me into a cage. I guess they figured I wouldn't be able to pull any of my Neanderthal tricks on them from in there. To my surprise, the cops who had been chasing me were already in the cage, so I guess I hadn't thrown them off the scent as completely as I had thought.

We spent four months there, with our keepers treating us as if we were brutal Neanderthals. We tried to convince them we were humans of great sophistication and cultural advancement, just like them, but they weren't buying it.

In the end we managed to escape by being brutally Neanderthal and bashing their overde-veloped heads in, getting so excited while we were doing it that we screamed and jumped around like monkeys. I'm not proud of that. It kind of makes their point that we were on a lower level than them mentally.

During our prolonged chase though time we accidentally altered the chronology of world history a little bit, I'm embarrassed to report. For example, the Civil War now happened BEFORE the Civil War. And when the Titanic sank it landed on the Bismarck. With Noah's Ark on top of the pile. Don't ask me how these things are possible. I just wreck history, I don't explain it. But I do know that this is what happens when sophisticated machinery like that is operated by unqualified personnel, like me.

The final stop in the chase was back in good old 1941. I jumped out of the elevator, clutching the battered figurine, and ducked down an alley. Thanks to my familiarity with the period, I managed to successfully elude their searches by hiding under the Andrews Sisters. The cops knew I would have to come back to the elevator sooner or later, so they finally decided to just wait there.

When I did go back to the elevator, I no longer had the figurine. And the Mark VI was no longer there. And Dodge and his boys were gone. While the 1941 cops were milling around trying to figure out why they were all out on the street together, with torn uniforms and bloody noses and foot long beards, I strolled past them into the elevator and headed for home.

CHAPTER TWENTY

I arrived safely back home in my own time, but due to being in a rush to get away from 1941, I had set some of the dials inaccurately. It was the correct date, but the location was slightly off. Instead of appearing on the sidewalk near my home, I appeared on Runway 35E at the airport.

I got out and looked around. It was going to be a long walk home. I decided to just correct the mistake I had made when I set the destination dials on the machine. I opened the briefcase and started fiddling with the dials and punching some buttons.

I guess I hit a wrong button somewhere and accidentally activated some special defense mechanism, because suddenly the briefcase started screaming. "Auto-destruct engaged!" it yelled wildly. "Glue applied to handle! Emitting poison gas! Die! Die! Everybody Die!"

I struggled with the briefcase for a moment, trying to get the damn thing to let go of me. Then I heard a growing roar and noticed that a jumbojet was about to land on me. To add to my problems, the briefcase was emitting noxious gas, ticking like a bomb, and cursing like a sailor. It was a situation that I had never been in, but I instinctively knew what to do. When in doubt, start breaking things.

Using all the burly strength at my command, I snapped off the handle, heaved the remainder of the briefcase as far out onto the runway as I could, then dove off to one side out of harm's way.

A few seconds later the time machine exploded with a disappointingly small thump. I wondered what it had been getting so excited about.

A moment later, several jumbojets touched down, one after the other, on the briefcase. Then an airport dog ran onto the runway, picked up the flattened briefcase and shook it. I went over, chased the dog off, then kicked what was left of the briefcase to pieces. It didn't make much sense, but I felt why am I the only person who doesn't get to wreck it?

When I got back to my house I took the figurine off the mantel and started to go back out. Halfway out the door I remembered that I probably should check in with Professor Groggins and let him know that I had kind of bunged up his time machine a little bit, and which runway he could scrape it off.

I put in a call to him and sketched out what had happened, trying to make the whole thing sound a little humorous, so maybe he'd decide he was kind of glad it had turned out the way it did because of the huge laugh he got out of it.

He didn't get the humor of the situation at all. I've got to work on my delivery, I guess. Timing is important too, darnit. Once he'd heard the whole story, the thing that worried him most was the possibility that I might have done something, maybe something that seemed inconsequential at the time, that might have altered history.

I admitted that during the police chase through time I had done a couple of things that I regarded as iffy. "I married my own mother and ran over myself as a small boy.

"What!"

"And I also stepped on something that was trying to evolve into me. But that was much earlier."

"Good God, man! Do you realize what this means? It means you were never born! You don't exist. Nothing you ever did in your life has happened now."

"Then how did I run over myself as a small boy?"

"Uh..."

"And if I don't exist, who are you talking to?"

After a moment's thought he said: "Look, I can show you the numbers, if you like."

I like science as much as the next guy, but this whole topic was starting to bore me. "I don't feel any different. What do I care about the paperwork? Anyway, I wrecked a lot more important stuff than my I.D. cards. Remind me to tell you about Ford's Theater."

Before I hung up I asked him to explain something that was puzzling me. Why was it that, after the past had been altered, we both still kind of remembered what it had been like before? Scientifically, how did that work?

Groggins confidently started to explain this phenomenon, but soon realized he had already gone way past what he actually knew on the subject, and was now in the magical realm of bullshit. At that point he stopped trying to explain it and just said he didn't know. So don't ask me how it works. But there's probably a simple explanation. You can probably find it in some other book.

A little later, I arrived at the gutter and handed Mandible the figurine. "Here you go, Chief."

Mandible delightedly grabbed the figurine and looked at it. It was a little the worse for wear, but it was his figurine all right. "I've got it! Now everything is back the way it was before and I'm rich again!"

He looked at the city skyline. All the museums and libraries were back, but there was something wrong. He couldn't identify what it was at first, but then the wind picked up a little bit and the rags he was wearing flapped in the breeze. He glanced down at his tattered clothes, then looked at me with a confused expression.

"What trickery is this? The city is back to the way it was, but I still seem to be poor. How is that possible?"

"You'll be even poorer when you pay my bill. My fee is $500 a day, as we discussed when you hired me. And even though only a couple of weeks have passed for you, I've been working on this case for over two years by my watch."

I handed him his bill and walked off. Mandible sat down on a heap of rubbish, took a long pull of some cheap wine, and started trying to figure out what had happened.

CHAPTER TWENTY-ONE

I got into my Rolls Royce, which was parked in front of the Burly Science Museum, drove past the Burly Library and the fabulous Burly Convention Center and pulled up to my office in the Burly Building. It's located on the corner of Burly and Burly, so it's an easy address to remember. All of the parking places in front of the building were reserved for me, so I could take my pick. Today I decided to park in the extra big one. I got out of the car, walked past the line of statues of me and went into the building.

I walked into my office, and looked around with satisfaction. All the photos and wise sayings I had on the wall were now framed in 14 carat gold. Neither one of my crappy chairs would ever fall over again now. I had used some of my vast wealth to get the leg on that one chair fixed.

My secretary was looking around the office, frowning, more confused than usual. On her head was a hat that was completely unknown to her.

"What happened to the office? It's different," she said. "And where did I get this hat?"

I sat back in my chair, confident that it wouldn't tip over, and gave her a quick summary of what I've told you, then told her what I hadn't told Mandible about my last visit to 1941.

I had wanted to use the figurine to get the city back to the way I remembered it, law abiding and peaceful, with no corrupt cops chasing me through time, but I didn't want Tom Mandible to get off Scot free. So on my last trip to 1941, I took the figurine to my grandfather and told him it was valuable evidence that he could use to blackmail the city's wealthy District Attorney. I said if he used it right he could make a fortune with it. The only condition was that he had to build libraries, museums etc, and stick my name prominently on each one.

It took awhile to explain all this to him, because we Burlys have never been very smart, but he finally got it. And once he understood the concept, he turned out to be a real first class blackmailer. He managed to bleed Tom Mandible so dry, that the D.A., infuriated at the way he was robbed of his ill-gotten gains, clamped down even harder on crime in the city. So the city ended up becoming even nicer and safer than it had been before.

Of course, nothing in life works perfectly. The Burly family was never very good with money, so the bulk of our family fortune got pissed away in one way or another, a lot of it in trying to blackmail other public officials with other figurines. But there was still a comfortable amount left over when I came along.

Elizabeth didn't believe very much of this story. It made me sound smart, which she knew I wasn't. But she liked the office better. And the hat was okay. So she didn't press the matter. She didn't have time to talk about it anymore today anyway. She had to go home now. That part in her hair was bothering her again.

I watched her go and got out a cigar. It's not often that I do something smart, but it happens sometimes, and when it does I like to celebrate. I started to light the cigar with a twenty dollar bill, then changed my mind and lit it with a stamp.

Then I noticed a stack of dust-covered correspondence on my desk that appeared to have been waiting there for me since 1941. There were overdue hotel bills, thank you notes from my grandfather and the Andrews Sisters, offers to join the "Wire Recorder Spool Of The Month Club" etc. I threw them all away. Too late to answer them now.

Then a very old dust-covered mechanic came into my office. It was that guy who had tried to build a time machine for me in 1941. I remembered now that I had never paid him. He remembered it too.

"You owe me 8 bucks," he said.

He held out a dust-covered bill. I examined it for a moment, then shrugged and paid him. It was only eight dollars. It would have cost more than that to fight him in court or hire someone to kill him. We rich guys always have to look at things from the financial angle. That's our curse.

He took the money and shuffled off, as happy as a really old guy with eight dollars can be.

Then a representative of our federal government showed up and presented me with a bill for WWII. I told him there must be some mistake. This bill couldn't be for me. This must be one of those rare instances, that comes along maybe once in a generation, when the government is full of shit.

He insisted it was a legitimate obligation, owed by me because of that telegram I hadn't sent. We did a lot of back and forth about "what telegram?" "you know what telegram!" for quite a while—I was starting to have a pretty good time—when I suddenly remembered what telegram he was talking about.

I had made several attempts during my stay in 1941 to send telegrams to the future. Every time someone new started working at the telegraph office, I gave it another try. But nothing ever came of it. One of the times, an agitated Japanese man was in line behind me. He was trying to get off an urgent telegram to the Imperial Japanese Fleet. He kept trying to move in front of me, but every time he did, I just gave him the old Burly Get-Back-There.

Finally he changed his tactics and tried to get me to send the message for him. He handed me the scrawled message. I took it, promised I would send it when I was done with what I was doing, unless I forgot about it, stuck the message in my pocket and forgot about it.

Now that I remembered the telegram, I was

curious as to what it said. I walked over to a trophy case that had, among other prized items, a pair of heavily worn trousers labeled "Time Travel Pants". I reached in the back pocket, pulled out the yellowed telegram and read it. It said "Don't Attack Pearl Harbor".

I walked back to my desk and looked over the itemized list of expenses I was being billed for. It said I was responsible for the loss of 139,000 tanks, 2800 ships, 268,000 airplanes, and was expected to pay for 60 million funerals.

I put the bill down and shook my head. "I admit I'm solely to blame for the war in the Pacific, but Hitler handled the European end of the thing, so he's at least as responsible for WWII as I am. Can't you bill him for some of these expenses?"

The government official shook his head. "He's dead."

"Shit."

We haggled for awhile, then I agreed to give them $80 a month until it was all paid off. I figured I got off easy.

I thought that tied up all the loose ends until Mandible came in one day with his tramp lawyer. They said they were suing me. I asked what for? The lawyer said I was liable for changing the course of human events in a way that was detrimental to his client. They had a pretty good case, being so right and everything, but I didn't think the case would ever get to trial. The tramp life had gotten to them both and pretty soon they had mostly forgotten about me and were fighting over my cigar butt. I gave them a bottle of cheap wine, then I waited until they were unconscious and settled the matter out of court by pushing them out of a window.

There's not too much left to tell. Professor Groggins, I've heard, is working on a machine that talks about the weather but doesn't do anything about it. That will save everybody a lot of time. At my request, he used his Mark VI time machine to go back in time and fix up most of the past that I had wrecked. He said there were a couple of things he couldn't change back, because I'd just screwed them up too bad. So if you're upset that we had a depression in the 1930's and that Richard Nixon was elected President twice, instead of being Lou Costello's partner in the movies, I guess you can blame me for that.

As for me personally, the only real change in my life, aside from the increase in my bank account, is that there are now fourteen of me living around town in different apartments. We avoid each other when we see each other on the street, maybe just a nod, but nothing more. It's a little unnerving, but doesn't seem to cause any harm otherwise. Except, of course, that now I've got a lot more competition in the detective business in this town. That's just what I need at this point.